GEORGES SIMENON

Maigret and the Hotel Majestic

Translated from the French
by Caroline Hillier

A Harvest Book
A Helen and Kurt Wolff Book
Harcourt Brace & Company
San Diego New York London

Requests for permission to make copies
of any part of the work should be mailed to:
Permissions Department, Harcourt Brace & Company,
6277 Sea Harbor Drive, Orlando, Florida 32887-6777.

Library of Congress Cataloging-in-Publication Data

Simenon, Georges.
Maigret and the Hotel Majestic.

This is a translation of Les caves du Majestic.
"A Helen and Kurt Wolff book."

I. Title

PZ3.S5892Maegk 1977b   [PQ2637.I53]
843'.9'12   77-84398
ISBN 0-15-655133-0

Printed in the United States of America
E F G H I J

1

Prosper Donge's Flat Tire

A car door slamming. The first thing he heard each day. The motor continued to run outside. Charlotte was probably saying good-by to the driver. Then the taxi drove off. Footsteps. The sound of the key in the lock and the click of the electric light switch.

A match was being struck in the kitchen, and he heard the slow "pfffttt" as the gas came alight.

Charlotte climbed slowly up the newly built staircase, having been on her feet all night. She crept noiselessly into the room. Another light switch. The light came on, through a pink handkerchief with wooden tassles at the corners that served as a makeshift shade.

Prosper Donge kept his eyes firmly closed. Charlotte undressed, glancing at herself in the wardrobe mirror. When she got to her bra and girdle, she sighed. She was as plump and pink as a Rubens, but had a passion for constricting herself. When she had finished undressing, she rubbed the bruise marks on her skin.

3

She had an irritating way of getting into the bed, kneeling on it first so that the mattress dipped to one side.

"Your turn, Prosper!"

He got up. She dived quickly into the warm hollow he had left, pulled the bedcovers up to her eyes, and lay there unmoving.

"Is it raining?" he asked, running water into the sink.

A muffled groan. It didn't matter. The water was icy, unfit for shaving. Trains rumbled past below.

Prosper Donge got dressed. Charlotte sighed from time to time, because she couldn't get to sleep with the light on. Just as he stretched out his right hand to the switch, with his other hand already on the doorknob, she muttered thickly:

"Don't forget to pay the installment for the radio."

There was hot coffee on the stove—too hot. He drank it standing up. Then, with the gestures of someone who does the same things every day, at the same time, he wrapped a knitted scarf around his neck, and put on his hat and coat.

Finally, he wheeled his bicycle along the hallway and out the door.

The air was always damp and cold at that hour of the morning, and the sidewalks were wet, although it hadn't rained; the people sleeping behind their closed shutters would probably waken to a warm, sunny day.

The street, with detached houses and little gardens on either side, ran steeply downhill. There was an occasional glimpse, through the trees, of the lights of Paris far down below.

It was no longer dark, but it wasn't yet light. The sky was bluish-mauve. Lights came on in a few windows, and Prosper Donge braked sharply as he reached the grade crossing, which was shut, and through which he passed by the side gates.

After the Pont de Saint-Cloud he turned left. A tugboat with its chain of barges was whistling angrily to be allowed into the lock.

4

The Bois de Boulogne . . . Lakes reflecting a whiter sky, with swans stirring awake . . .

As he reached the Porte Dauphine, Donge suddenly felt the ground become harder under his wheels. He went on a few yards, jumped off, and saw that his back tire was flat.

He checked the time by his watch. It was ten to six. He started to walk quickly, pushing his bike, and his breath hung in the air as he panted along, with a burning sensation in his chest from the effort.

Avenue Foch . . . The shutters of the private houses were all still closed. . . . Only an officer trotting along the bridle path, followed by his orderly.

Getting lighter behind the Arc de Triomphe. He was hurrying along, feeling very hot now.

At the corner of the Champs-Elysées, a policeman in a cape, near the newspaper kiosk, called out:

"Flat tire?"

He nodded. Only three hundred yards more. The Hotel Majestic, on the left, had all its windows still shuttered. The street lamps barely shed any light now.

He turned up Rue de Berri, then Rue de Ponthieu. A small café-bar was open. And two houses farther along, there was a door that passers-by never noticed, the service entrance of the Majestic.

A man was coming out. He appeared to be in evening dress under his gray overcoat. He was bareheaded. His hair was plastered down, and Prosper Donge thought it was Zebio, the dancer.

He could have glanced into the bar to see if he was right, but it didn't occur to him to do so. Still pushing his bike, he started down the long gray corridor, lighted by a single lamp. He stopped at the time clock, punched in at his number, 67, his eyes on the little clock, which said ten past six. Click.

It was now established that he had arrived at the Majestic at 6:10 A.M.—ten minutes later than usual.

That was the official statement made by Prosper Donge, breakfast cook at the Champs-Elysée hotel.

He had gone on to do what he did on any other morning, he said.

At that hour, the vast basement, with its twisting corridors, innumerable doors, and gray-painted walls like those of a ship's gangway, was deserted. Here and there you could see a feeble light from a yellowish bulb—all the light there was at night—shining through the glass partitions.

There were glass partitions everywhere, with the kitchens on the left, and the pastry cook's kitchen beyond. Opposite was the room called the personnel dining room, where the senior staff and the guests' own servants, personal maids, and chauffeurs had their meals. Farther on was the junior-staff dining room, with long wooden tables and benches like those in a school.

Finally, overlooking the basement like a captain's bridge, there was a smaller glass cage, where the bookkeeper kept a check on everything that left the kitchens.

As he opened the door of the breakfast kitchen, Prosper Donge had the impression that someone was going up the narrow staircase that led to the upper floors, but he didn't pay any special attention at the time. Or so he stated later, in his deposition.

He struck a match, just as Charlotte had done in their little house, and the gas went "pffftt" under the smallest percolator, which he heated first for the few guests who got up early.

Only when he had done this did he go to the cloakroom. It was a fairly large room, down one of the corridors. There were several washbasins, a grayish mirror, and tall, narrow metal lockers around the walls, each with a number.

6

He opened locker 67 with his key, took off his coat, hat, and scarf, and changed his shoes; he liked wearing softer, more flexible shoes when he worked. He put on a white jacket.

A few minutes to go . . . At half past six, the basement burst into life.

Upstairs, they were all still asleep, except the night concierge, who was waiting to be relieved in the deserted lobby.

The percolator whistled. Donge filled a cup with coffee and started up the staircase, which was like one of those mysterious staircases in the wings of a theater that lead to the most unexpected places.

Pushing open a narrow door, he found himself in the lobby cloakroom; no one would have known that the door, covered by a large mirror, was there.

"Coffee!" he announced, putting the cup on the cloakroom counter. "Everything OK?"

"OK!" the night concierge grunted, coming to get the coffee.

Donge went downstairs again. His three women helpers, the Three Fatties, as they were called, had arrived. They were tough ladies, all three ugly, and one of them old and cantankerous. They were already noisily clanking cups and saucers in the sink.

Donge continued his daily routine, ranging the silver-plated coffeepots in order of size—one, two, or three cups. Then the little creamers, teapots, and so on.

He caught sight of Jean Ramuel, looking disheveled, in the bookkeeper's glass booth.

"Spent the night here again!" he said to himself.

For the past three or four nights, Ramuel, the bookkeeper, had slept at the hotel, instead of going home to Montparnasse.

Officially, this was not allowed. There was a room with four beds at the end of the corridor, near the door leading to the wine cellers. But in theory the beds were meant for the use of staff

7

members who needed to rest between busy times during their duty periods.

Donge waved his hand in greeting to Ramuel, who responded equally casually.

Then it was time for the head chef—vast and full of pomp—to arrive back from the market with his van, which he parked on Rue de Ponthieu for his assistants to unload.

By half past seven there were at least thirty people scurrying around in the basement of the Majestic, and bells began to ring, dumbwaiters began to descend, to be loaded before ascending with their trays, while Ramuel speared pink, blue, and white slips of paper on the metal prongs on his desk.

Then it was time for the day concierge, in his light-blue uniform, to take up his position in the lobby, and for the mail clerk to sort the letters in his little cubbyhole. The sun was probably shining out on the Champs-Elysées, but down in the basement they were aware only of the buses rumbling overhead, making the glass partitions tremble.

At a few minutes past nine—at four minutes past nine precisely, it was later established—Prosper Donge came out of his breakfast kitchen, and, a few seconds later, went into the cloakroom.

"I had left my handkerchief in my coat pocket . . ." he stated when interrogated.

At all events, he found himself alone in the room with its hundred metal lockers. Did he open his? There were no witnesses. Did he look for his handkerchief? Possibly he did.

There were actually not a hundred, but only ninety-two lockers, all numbered. The last five were empty.

Why did it occur to Prosper Donge to open locker 89, which wasn't assigned to anyone and was therefore not locked?

"It was automatic . . ." he said later. "The door was

8

open. . . . I wasn't thinking. . . ."

In the locker was a body that had been pushed in upright and had fallen over on itself. It was the body of a woman of about thirty, very blonde—peroxided blonde, in fact—wearing a dress of fine black wool.

Donge didn't cry out. He turned very pale, and, going up to Ramuel's glass cage, bent to whisper through the grille.

"Come here a minute. . . ."

The bookkeeper followed him.

"Stay there. . . . Don't let anyone in. . . ."

Ramuel bounded up the stairs, burst into the lobby cloakroom, and saw the concierge talking to a chauffeur.

"Is the manager here yet?"

The concierge gestured with his chin toward the manager's office.

Maigret paused outside the revolving door. He was about to tap his pipe on his heel to empty it, then shrugged, and put it back in his mouth. It was his first pipe of the day—the best.

"The manager is expecting you, Superintendent. . . ."

There were few signs of life in the foyer as yet. An Englishman was arguing with the mail clerk, and a young girl walked through on grasshopper-long legs, carrying a hatbox that she had probably come to deliver.

Maigret went into the office, and the manager shook his hand silently and pointed to a chair. There was a green curtain across the glass door, but if one pulled it back a little, one could see everything that went on.

"A cigar?"

"No, thank you . . ."

They had known each other for a long time. There was no need to say much. The manager was wearing striped trousers, a black jacket, and a tie that seemed to have been cut from some rigid material.

"Here . . ."

He pushed a registration form toward his visitor.

"Oswald J. Clark, industrialist, of Detroit, Michigan (U.S.A.). Traveling from Detroit.

"Arrived on February 12.

"Accompanied by Mrs. Clark, his wife; Teddy Clark, aged 7, his son; Ellen Darroman, aged 24, governess; Gertrud Borms, aged 42, maid.

"Suite 203."

The telephone rang. The manager answered impatiently. Maigret folded the form in four and put it in his wallet.

"Which of them is it?"

"Mrs. Clark . . ."

"Ah!"

"The hotel doctor, whom I telephoned as soon as I had informed the police, and who lives just around the corner on Rue de Berri, is already here. He says Mrs. Clark was strangled some time between six and six-thirty in the morning."

The manager was dismal. There was no need to tell an old hand like Maigret that it was a disaster for the hotel, and that if there was any way of hushing it up . . .

"The Clark family has been here a week, then . . ." murmured the Superintendent. "What sort of people are they?"

"Well heeled . . . Very much so . . . He's a tall, thin, silent American, about forty . . . forty-five, perhaps. . . . His wife—poor thing—seems to be French. Twenty-eight or twenty-nine . . . I didn't see very much of her. The governess is pretty. The maid, who also looks after the child, is really common and foul-tempered. Ah! . . . I nearly forgot to tell you. . . . Clark left for Rome yesterday morning. . . ."

"Alone?"

"From what I can gather, he is in Europe on business. He has a ball-bearing factory. He has to visit various European capitals, and he decided to leave his wife, son, and staff in Paris for the time being."

"What train did he take?" Maigret asked.

The manager picked up the telephone.

"Concierge? What train did Mr. Clark take yesterday? . . . Suite 203, yes . . . Wasn't there any luggage to take to the station? He only took a small bag? By taxi? . . . Désiré's taxi? . . . Thank you . . .

"Did you get that, Superintendent? He left at eleven o'clock yesterday morning in a taxi, Désiré's taxi, which is nearly always parked outside the hotel. He took only one small bag with him. . . ."

"Do you mind if I make a call myself? . . . Hello! Police Headquarters, please, mademoiselle . . . Police Headquarters? . . . Lucas? Get over to the Gare de Lyon. Check on the trains to Rome from eleven yesterday morning."

He continued to give instructions, while his pipe went out.

"Tell Torrence to find Désiré's taxi. . . . It's usually outside the Majestic. Find out where he took a fare, a tall, thin American he picked up outside the hotel yesterday. . . . That's it. . . ."

He looked for an ashtray in which to empty his pipe. The manager handed him one.

"Are you sure you won't have a cigar? The nursemaid is in a great state. . . . I thought it best to tell her. And the governess didn't sleep at the hotel last night. . . ."

"What floor is the suite on?"

"On the second floor. Looking out over the Champs-Elysées. Mr. Clark's room, separated from his wife's by a sitting room;

then the child's room, the maid's, and the governess's. They wanted to be all in one suite."

"Has the night concierge left?"

"He can be reached by telephone. His wife is the concierge of a new apartment house in Neuilly. Hello! . . . Can you get me . . ."

Five minutes later they knew that Mrs. Clark had gone to the theater alone the evening before, and that she had got back a few minutes past midnight. The nursemaid had not gone out. The governess, on the other hand, had not dined at the hotel and had been out all night.

"Shall we go downstairs and have a look?" Maigret said with a sigh.

The lobby was busier now, but no one was aware of the drama that had occurred while they were still sleeping.

"We'll go this way. . . . I'll lead the way, Superintendent."

As he spoke, the manager frowned. Someone was entering the lobby through the revolving door, letting in a shaft of sunlight. A young woman in a gray suit came in, and as she passed the mail desk, she asked:

"Anything for me?"

"That's her, Superintendent—Miss Ellen Darroman. . . ."

Fine silk stockings, with straight seams. The well-groomed look of someone who had dressed with care. She didn't appear tired at all, and the brisk February air had brought color to her cheeks.

"Do you want to talk to her?"

"Not yet . . . Wait a minute. . . ."

And Maigret went over to an inspector he had brought along who was standing in a corner of the lobby.

"Don't let that girl out of your sight. . . . If she goes into her room, watch outside the door."

12

The cloakroom. The tall mirror turned on its hinges. The Superintendent followed the manager down the narrow staircase. A sudden end to all the gilt, potted plants, and elegant bustle. A smell of cooking rose to meet them.

"Does this staircase go to all the floors?"

"There are two of them, leading from the basement to the attics. But you have to know your way around to use them. For instance, upstairs, there are small doors exactly like the other doors, but without numbers. None of the visitors would ever guess. . . ."

It was nearly eleven o'clock. There were not fifty, but more like a hundred and fifty people now, scurrying around in the basement, some in white chefs' hats, others in waiters' coats, or cellarmen's aprons, and the women, like Prosper Donge's Three Fatties, doing the dirty work. . . .

"This way . . . Watch out so you don't get dirty or slip. . . . The hallways are very narrow."

Everyone stared at them through the glass partitions, particularly at the Superintendent. Jean Ramuel was busy catching each slip handed up to him as its bearer flew past, and casting an eagle eye over the contents of the trays.

It was a shock to see the unexpected figure of a policeman standing on guard outside the cloakroom. The doctor—a very young man—had been warned that Maigret was coming, and stood there waiting, smoking a cigarette.

"Shut the door. . . ."

The body was lying on the floor in the middle of the room, surrounded by the metal lockers. The doctor, still smoking, muttered:

"She must have been attacked from behind. . . . She didn't struggle for very long. . . ."

"And her body wasn't dragged over the floor," Maigret

13

added, examining the dead woman's black clothes. "There are no traces of dust. Either the crime was committed here, or she was carried, by two people probably, because it would be difficult in this labyrinth of narrow corridors. . . ."

There was an alligator handbag in the locker where she had been found. The Superintendent opened it and took out an automatic, which he slipped into his pocket, after checking whether the safety catch was on. There was nothing else in the bag except a handkerchief, a powder compact, and a few bank notes amounting to less than a thousand francs.

Behind them, it was humming like a beehive. The dumbwaiters shot up and down, bells rang ceaselessly, and they could see heavy copper saucepans being wielded behind the glass partitions of the kitchens, and chickens being roasted by the dozen.

"Everything must be left untouched for the Public Prosecutor's Department," Maigret said. "Who found the body?"

Prosper Donge was pointed out to him. He was cleaning a percolator. He was tall, with the kind of red hair usually referred to as carroty. He looked somewhere between forty-five and forty-eight. His eyes were blue, his face badly pockmarked.

"Has he been here long?"

"Five years. Before that he was at the Miramar, in Cannes."

"Reliable?"

"Extremely reliable."

There was a partition separating Donge and the Superintendent. Their eyes met through the glass. And a rush of color flooded the face of the breakfast cook, who, like all redheads, had sensitive skin.

"Excuse me, sir. . . . Superintendent Maigret is wanted on the telephone."

It was Jean Ramuel, the bookkeeper, who had hurried out of his cage.

"If you'd like to take the call here . . ."

A message from Headquarters. There had only been two express trains to Rome since eleven o'clock the day before. Oswald J. Clark had not traveled on either of them. And the taxi driver Désiré, whom they had managed to reach by telephone at a bistro where he was one of the regulars, swore he had taken his fare, the day before, to the Hotel Aiglon, on Boulevard Montparnasse.

Voices came from the staircase, one of them the high-pitched voice of a young woman protesting in English to a *valet de chambre* who was trying to bar her way.

It was the governess, Ellen Darroman, who was bearing down on them.

2

Maigret Goes Bicycling

Pipe in mouth, bowler on the back of his head, and hands in the pockets of his vast overcoat with the famous velvet collar, Maigret watched her arguing vehemently with the hotel manager.

And one glance at the Superintendent's face made it clear that there would not be much sympathy lost between him and Ellen Darroman.

"What's she saying?" he sighed, interrupting, unable to understand a single word the American woman said.

"She wants to know if it's true Mrs. Clark has been murdered, and if anyone has telephoned Rome to let Oswald J. Clark know; she wants to know where the body has been taken and if . . ."

But the girl didn't let him finish. She had listened impatiently, frowning, had thrown Maigret a cold glance, and had gone on talking faster than ever.

"What's she saying?"

"She wants me to show her the body and . . ."

Maigret gently took the American girl's arm, to guide her

toward the cloakroom. But he knew she would shy away from the contact. Just the kind of woman who exasperated him in American movies! A terrifyingly brisk walk. All the kitchen staff were gaping at her through the glass partitions.

"Do come in," murmured the Superintendent, not without irony.

She took three steps forward, saw the body wrapped in a blanket on the floor, remained stock still, and started jabbering away in English again.

"What's she saying?"

"She wants us to uncover the body. . . ."

Maigret complied, without taking his eyes off her. He saw her start, then immediately recover her composure, in spite of the horrifying nature of what she saw.

"Ask her if she recognizes Mrs. Clark. . . ."

A shrug. A particularly disagreeable way of tapping her high heel on the floor.

"What's she saying?"

"That you know as well as she does."

"In that case, please ask her to go up to your office, and tell her that I have a few questions to ask her."

The manager translated. Maigret took this opportunity to cover the dead woman's face again.

"What's she saying?"

"She says no."

"Really? Kindly inform her of my position as head of the Homicide Squad."

Ellen, who was looking straight at him, spoke without waiting for this to be translated. And Maigret repeated his interminable:

"What's she saying?"

"What's she saying?" she repeated, mimicking him, overcome by unjustifiable irritation.

And she spoke in English again, as if to herself.

"Translate what she's saying for me, will you?"

"She says that . . . that she knows perfectly well you're from the police . . . that . . ."

"Speak up!"

"That one has only to see you with your hat on and your pipe in your mouth . . . I'm sorry . . . you asked me to tell you. . . . She says she won't go up to my office and that she won't answer your questions. . . ."

"Why not?"

"I'll ask her. . . ."

Ellen Darroman, who was lighting a cigarette, listened to the manager's question, shrugged again, and snapped a few words.

"She says she's under no obligation to answer and that she will only obey an official summons. . . ."

At this the girl threw a last look at Maigret, turned on her heel, and walked, with the same decisive air, toward the staircase.

The manager turned somewhat anxiously toward the Superintendent, and was amazed to see that he was smiling.

He had had to take off his overcoat, because of the heat in the basement, but he hadn't abandoned his bowler, or his pipe. Thus accoutered, he wandered peacefully along the corridors, his hands behind his back, stopping from time to time by one of the glass partitions, somewhat as if he were inspecting an aquarium.

The huge basement, with its electric lights burning all day long, did in fact strike him as being very much like an oceanographic museum. In each glass cage there were creatures, varying in number, darting to and fro. You could see them constantly appearing and disappearing, heavily laden, carrying saucepans or piles of plates, setting dumbwaiters or service elevators in motion, forever using little instruments, the telephones.

21

"What would someone from another planet make of it all?"

The visit from the Public Prosecutor's Department had lasted only a few minutes, and the examining magistrate had given Maigret a free hand, as usual. The latter had made several telephone calls from Jean Ramuel's bookkeeper's cage.

Ramuel's nose was set so crookedly that one always seemed to be viewing him in profile. And he looked as though he were suffering from a liver complaint. When his lunch was brought to him on a tray, he took a glassine bag of white powder from his vest pocket and dissolved its contents in a glass of water.

Between one and three o'clock, the pace was at its most hectic, everything happening so fast that it was like seeing a movie run off in fast motion.

"Excuse me. . . . Sorry . . ."

People were constantly bumping into the Superintendent, who continued his walk unperturbed, stopping and starting, asking a question now and then.

How many people had he talked to? At least twenty, he reckoned. The head chef had explained to him how the kitchens were run. Jean Ramuel had told him what the various colors of the slips of paper signified.

And he had watched—always through the glass partitions—the guests' servants having their lunch. Gertrud Borms, the Clarks' nursemaid, had come down. She was a large, hard-faced woman.

"Does she speak French?"

"Not a word . . ."

She had eaten heartily, chatting to a liveried chauffeur who sat. opposite her.

But what amazed him most of all was the sight of Prosper Donge, all this time, in his kitchen. He looked exactly like a large goldfish in a bowl. His hair was a fiery red. He had the almost

22

brick-red complexion redheads sometimes have, and his lips were thick and fishlike.

And he looked exactly like a fish when he came to press his face up against the glass, with his great, round, bewildered eyes, probably worried because the Superintendent hadn't spoken to him yet.

Maigret had questioned everyone. But he had hardly seemed to notice Prosper Donge's presence, although it was he who had discovered the body, and he was therefore the principal witness.

Donge, too, had his lunch, at a little table in his kitchen, while his three women bustled around him. A bell would ring about once a minute to indicate that the dumbwaiter was coming down. It arrived at a sort of hatch. Donge seized the slip of paper on it, and replaced it with the order on a tray, and the dumbwaiter rose again to one of the upper floors.

All these seemingly complicated operations were in fact quite simple. The large dining room of the Majestic, where two or three hundred people would then be having lunch, was immediately above the kitchens, so most of the dumbwaiters went there. Each time one of them came down again, it brought with it the sound of music.

Some of the guests had their meals in their rooms, however, and there was a waiter for each floor. There was also a tearoom on the same level as the basement, with dancing in the afternoons, from about five o'clock.

The men from the Forensic Laboratory had come for the body, and two specialists from the Criminal Records Office had spent half an hour working on locker 89 with cameras and powerful lights, looking for fingerprints.

None of this seemed to interest Maigret. They would be sure to inform him of the results in due course.

Watching him, one would have thought an amateur was studying how a grand hotel functions. He went up the narrow staircase, opened a door, then immediately closed it again, because it led to the large dining room, which was filled with the sound of clinking cutlery, music, and conversation.

He went up to the next floor. A corridor, with doors numbered to infinity and a red carpet stretching into the distance.

It was obvious that any of the guests could open the door and make his way to the basement. The same applied to the entrance on Rue de Ponthieu. Two bellboys and a concierge guarded the revolving door at the Champs-Elysées entry, but any stray passer-by could get into the Majestic by using the service entrance, and probably no one would notice him.

The same is true of most theaters. They are rigorously guarded at the front, but wide open at the stage-door side.

From time to time people went into the cloakroom in their working clothes. Shortly afterward they could be seen leaving, smartly dressed, in their hats and coats.

They were going off duty. The head chef went to the back room for a nap, which he did every day betweeen the lunch and dinner shifts.

Soon after four there was a loud burst of music, from the neighboring tearoom, and the dancing began. Prosper Donge, looking exhausted, filled rows of minute teapots and microscopic creamers, and then came anxiously up to the glass partition once more, casting nervous glances in Maigret's direction.

At five o'clock his three women went off duty and were replaced by two others. At six he took a wad of bills and a sheet of paper, obviously his accounts for the day, to Jean Ramuel. Then he in turn went into the cloakroom, came out in his street clothes, and fetched his bicycle, the flat tire having been repaired by one of the bellboys.

Outside it was now dark. Rue de Ponthieu was congested.

24

Prosper Donge made for the Champs-Elysées, weaving his way between taxis and buses. When he was almost at the Etoile, he suddenly did an about-face, bicycled back to Rue de Ponthieu, and went into a radio shop, where he handed over three hundred-odd francs to the cashier as one of the monthly installments he had contracted to pay.

Back to the Champs-Elysées. Then on to the regal calm of Avenue Foch, with only an occasional car gliding silently past. He pedaled slowly, with the air of one who has a long way to go yet—an honest citizen pedaling along the same route at the same time every day.

A voice came from behind, speaking quite close to him:

"I hope you don't mind, Monsieur Donge, if I go the rest of the way with you?"

He braked so violently that he skidded, and almost collided with Maigret on his bicycle. For it was Maigret who was bicycling along beside him, on a bike that he had borrowed from a bellboy at the Majestic and that was too small for him.

"I can't think," Maigret continued, "why everyone who lives in the suburbs doesn't go by bicycle. It's much more healthy and agreeable than going by bus or train!"

They were entering the Bois de Boulogne. Soon they saw the shimmer of street lights reflected in the lake.

"You were so busy all day that I didn't want to disturb you in your work. . . ."

And Maigret, too, was pedaling along with the regular rhythm of someone who is used to bicycling. Now and then there was the click of a gear.

"Do you know what Jean Ramuel did before he came to the Majestic?"

"He was a bank accountant. . . . The Atoum Bank, on Rue Caumartin . . ."

"Ah—the Atoum Bank . . . Doesn't sound too good to me . . . Don't you think he has a rather shifty look about him?"

"He's not in very good health," Prosper Donge mumbled.

"Watch out . . . you nearly struck the sidewalk. There's something else I'd like to ask you, if you won't think it impertinent. . . . You're the breakfast cook. Well, I was wondering what made you take up that profession. I mean . . . I mean it isn't something one suddenly feels a calling for, one doesn't say to oneself at fifteen or sixteen, 'I'm going to be a breakfast cook. . . .'"

"Watch out . . . if you swerve like that you'll get run down by a car. . . . You were saying?"

Donge explained, in a dejected voice, that he had been a foster child, and that until he was fifteen he had lived on a farm near Vitry-le-François. Then he had gone to work in a café in the town, first as an errand boy, and then as a waiter.

"After doing my military service, I wasn't very fit, and I wanted to live in the south of France. I was a waiter in Marseilles, and Cannes. Then they decided, at the Miramar, that I didn't look right to wait tables. . . . I looked 'awkward,' was the word the manager used. I was put in the breakfast kitchen. I was there for years, and then I took the job of breakfast cook at the Majestic."

They were crossing the Pont de Saint-Cloud. After turning down two or three narrow streets they reached the bottom of a fairly steep incline, and Prosper Donge got off his bike.

"Are you coming any farther?" he asked.

"If you don't mind. After spending a day in the hotel basement, I can appreciate even more your wish to live in the country. Do you do any gardening?"

"A little."

"Flowers?"

"Flowers and vegetables."

Now they were going up a badly surfaced, badly lighted street, pushing their bicycles; their breath came more quickly, and they didn't talk much.

"Do you know what I discovered while I was nosing around in the basement and talking to everyone I could see? That three people, at least, slept in the hotel basement last night. First, Jean Ramuel . . . It appears . . . it's rather amusing . . . it appears that he has an impossibly difficult mistress and that she periodically shuts him out of the house. For the last three or four days she's done it again, and he's been sleeping at the Majestic. Does the manager know?"

"It's not officially allowed, but he turns a blind eye. . . ."

"The professional dancing partner slept there, too . . . the one you call Zebio. A strange fellow, isn't he? At first sight, he seems too good to be true. He's called Eusebio Fualdès on the studio portraits in the tearoom. Then, when you read his identity papers, you discover that, in spite of his dark skin, he was born in Lille, and that his real name is Edgar Fagonet. There was a dance last night, in honor of a film star. He was around until half past three in the morning. It seems that he's so poor that he decided to sleep at the hotel, rather than get a taxi."

Prosper Donge had stopped, near a lamppost, and stood there, his face scarlet, his expression anxious.

"What are you doing?" Maigret asked.

"I'm home. . . . I . . ."

Light filtered out under the door of a little detached house of ground stone.

"Would it bother you if I came in for a moment?"

Maigret could have sworn that the great oaf's legs were trembling, that his throat was constricted, and that he felt ready to faint. He finally managed to stutter:

"Not at all."

He opened the door with his key, pushed his bike into the hall, and announced, in what was probably his usual way: "It's me!"

There was a glass door at the end of the hallway, leading to the kitchen; the light was on. Donge went in.

"This is . . ."

Charlotte was sitting by the stove, her feet on the hob, and was sewing a shrimp-pink silk petticoat, lolling in her chair.

She looked embarrassed, took her feet off the stove, and tried to find her slippers under the chair.

"Oh! There's someone with you. . . . Please excuse me, monsieur."

A cup with some dregs of coffee was on the table, and a plate with some cake crumbs.

"Come in. . . . Sit down. . . . Prosper hardly ever brings anyone home."

It was hot. The radio—a new one—was on. Charlotte was in her dressing gown, her stockings rolled down below the knee.

"Police officer? What's going on?" she asked anxiously, when Donge introduced Maigret.

"Nothing, madame . . . I happened to be working at the Majestic today, and I met your husband there."

At the word "husband," she looked at Prosper and burst out laughing.

"Did he tell you we were married?"

"I just thought . . ."

"Not at all! Sit down. We're just living together. I think we're really more like friends than anything else. Aren't we, Prosper? We've known each other so long! . . . Mind you, if I wanted him to marry me . . . But as I always tell him, what difference would it make? Everyone who knows me knows I was a dancer, and then a night-club hostess, on the Riviera. And that if I hadn't got so fat, I wouldn't have needed to work in the cloakroom in a club on

28

Rue Fontaine. Oh, Prosper, did you think to make the payment on the radio?''

"It's all done.''

An agricultural program was announced on the radio, and Charlotte switched it off, noticed that her dressing gown was open, and pinned it together with a large safety pin. Some leftovers were heating in a pan on the stove. Charlotte wondered whether to set the table. And Prosper Donge didn't know what to do with himself or where to go.

"We could go into the living room,'' he suggested.

"You forget there's no fire there . . . you'll freeze! If you two want to talk, I can go upstairs and get dressed. You see, Superintendent, we play a sort of game of musical chairs. When I get back, he goes out; when he gets back it's almost time for me to leave, and we just about have time to have something to eat together. And even our days off hardly ever seem to coincide, so that when he has a free day he has to get his own lunch. Would you like a drink? . . . Can you get him something, Prosper? . . . I'll go upstairs.''

Maigret hurriedly interrupted:

"No, no, madame . . . do please stay. I'm leaving right away. . . . You see, a crime was committed this morning, at the Majestic. I wanted to ask your . . . your friend a few questions, as the crime occurred in the basement, at a time when he was almost the only person down there.''

He had to make an effort to continue the cruel game, because Donge's face—did he look like a fish, or was it a sheep?—expressed so much painful anguish. He was trying to keep calm. He almost succeeded. But at the cost of how much inner turmoil?

Only Charlotte seemed unmoved, as she calmly poured out drinks in small, gold-rimmed glasses.

29

"Something to do with one of the staff?" she said with surprise, but still unperturbed.

"In the basement, but not one of the staff . . . That is what is so puzzling about the whole affair. Imagine to yourself a hotel guest, from one of the luxury suites, staying at the Majestic with her husband, her son, a nursemaid, and a governess. . . . A suite costing more than a thousand francs a day . . . Well, at six o'clock in the morning she is strangled, not in her room, but in the cloakroom in the basement. In all probability, the crime was committed there. What was the woman doing in the basement? Who had lured her down there, and why? Especially at a time when people of that sort are usually still fast asleep . . ."

It was barely noticeable: a slight knitting of the brows, as if an idea had occurred to Charlotte and was immediately dismissed. A quick glance at Prosper, who was warming his hands over the stove. He had very white hands, with square fingers, covered with red hairs.

But Maigret continued relentlessly:

"It won't be easy to find out what this Mrs. Clark had come down to the basement for. . . ."

He held his breath, forced himself to remain motionless, to look as if he were studying the oilcloth on the table. You could have heard a pin drop.

Maigret seemed to be trying to give Charlotte time to regain her composure. She had frozen. Her mouth was half open, but no words came out. Then they heard her make a vague noise that sounded like "Ah!"

Too bad! It was his job. His duty.

"I was wondering if you knew her. . . ."

"Me?"

"Not by the name of Mrs. Clark, under which she has been known for the last six years only, but by the name of Emilienne,

30

or, rather, Mimi . . . She was a hostess, in Cannes, at the time when . . ."

Poor plump Charlotte! What a bad actress she was. Scanning the ceiling as if she were racking her memory. Staring with wide-eyed innocence.

"Emilienne? . . . Mimi? . . . No! I don't think . . . You're sure it was Cannes?"

"In a club that was then called La Belle Etoile, just behind the Croisette . . ."

"It's strange. . . . I don't recall a Mimi. . . . Do you, Prosper?"

It was a miracle he didn't choke. What was the point of forcing him to talk, when he was literally strangling?

"N-no . . ."

Nothing had outwardly changed. There was still that pleasant, homely smell in the kitchen, the walls of the little house exuding a reassuring warmth, still the familiar smell of meat braising on a bed of golden onions. The red-and-white-checked oilcloth on the table. Cake crumbs. Like most women who have a tendency to grow fat, Charlotte probably went in for orgies of solitary cake eating.

And the shrimp-pink silk petticoat!

Then, suddenly, the tension evaporated, for no apparent reason. Someone coming in would probably have thought that the Donge family was quietly entertaining a neighbor.

Only none of them dared say a word. The unfortunate Prosper, his skin pitted like a sieve with pockmarks, had shut his periwinkle-blue eyes and was standing, swaying, by the stove, looking as though he would fall on the kitchen floor at any moment.

Maigret got up with a sigh.

"I'm so sorry to have disturbed you. . . . It's time I . . ."

31

"I'll come to the door with you," Charlotte said quickly. "It's time I got dressed, anyway. . . . I have to be there at ten, and there's only one bus every hour in the evening. So . . ."

"Good night, Donge . . ."

"Good . . ."

Possibly he said the rest, but they didn't hear him. Maigret found his bicycle outside. She shut the door. He nearly looked through the keyhole, but someone was coming down the road, and he didn't want to be caught in that position.

He braked all the way down the hill, and stopped in front of a bistro.

"Can you keep this bicycle for me, if I send for it tomorrow morning?"

He swallowed the first thing that came to hand and went to wait for the bus at the Pont de Saint-Cloud. For more than an hour Police Sergeant Lucas would have been telephoning frantically, trying in vain to locate his boss.

3

Charlotte at the "Pélican"

"There you are at last, Monsieur Maigret!"

Standing in the doorway of his apartment on Boulevard Richard-Lenoir, the Superintendent couldn't help smiling, not because his wife called him "Monsieur Maigret," which she often did when she was joking, but at the warm smell that came to meet him and that reminded him . . .

It was a long way from Saint-Cloud, and he lived in a very different setting from that of the unmarried Donge couple. But still—on his return he found Madame Maigret sewing, not in the kitchen, but in the dining room, her feet not on the hob but on the dining-room stove. And he could have sworn that here, too, there were some cake crumbs tucked away somewhere.

A hanging lamp above the round table. A cloth with a large, round soup tureen in the middle, a carafe of wine, a carafe of water, and table napkins in round silver rings. The smell coming from the kitchen was exactly the same as that from the Donges' stew. . . .

"They've called three times."

"From the House?"

That was what he and his colleagues sometimes called Police Headquarters.

He took off his coat with a sigh of relief, warmed his hands over the stove for a minute, and remembered that Prosper Donge had done exactly the same thing a short while ago. Then he picked up the receiver and dialed a number.

"Is that you, Chief?" asked Lucas's kindly voice at the other end of the line. "All right? . . . Anything new? . . . I've got one or two small things to report, that's why I'm still here. First, about the governess . . .

"Janvier has been shadowing her since she left the Majestic. Do you know what Janvier says about her? He says that in her country she must be a gangster, not a governess. . . .

"Hello! . . . Well, I'll give you a brief rundown on what happened. . . . She left the hotel soon after talking to you. Instead of taking the taxi the doorman had called for her, she jumped into a taxi that was passing by, and Janvier had to scurry not to lose her.

"When they got to the Grands Boulevards, she rushed down into the métro, then twice doubled back on her tracks. Janvier didn't give up, and followed her to the Gare de Lyon. He was afraid she might take a train, since he didn't have enough money on him.

"The Rome Express was to leave from Platform Four—in ten minutes' time. Ellen Darroman looked in all the compartments. Just as she was turning back, disappointed, a tall, very elegant man arrived, carrying a bag."

"Oswald J. Clark," said Maigret, who was looking vaguely at his wife as he listened. "She obviously wanted to warn him. . . ."

"According to Janvier, it appears that they greeted each other much more like intimate friends than like employer and employee. Have you seen Clark? He's a tall, lanky devil; muscular, with the open, healthy face of a baseball player. They went along the platform arguing, as if Clark were still thinking of leaving. When the train started, he still hadn't made up his mind, because it looked for a minute as though he were going to jump onto the train.

"Then they left the station. They hailed a taxi. A few minutes later they were at the American Embassy, on Avenue Gabriel. . . .

"Next they went to Avenue Friedland, to see a lawyer.

"The lawyer telephoned the examining magistrate, and three quarters of an hour later, all three of them arrived at the Palais de Justice and were taken at once to the magistrate's office. . . .

"I don't know what went on inside, but the magistrate wanted you to call him as soon as you got back. It seems it's very urgent.

"To conclude Janvier's story, after leaving the Palais de Justice, our three characters went to the Forensic Laboratory to identify the body officially. Then they went back to the Majestic, and there Clark had two whiskies in the bar with the lawyer, while the young woman went up to her room.

"That's all, Chief. The magistrate seems very anxious to have a word with you. What time is it? He'll be at home until eight; Turbigo 25–62. Then he's having dinner with some friends, whose number he gave me. Just a minute . . . Galvani 47–53.

"Anything more you need me for, Chief? Good night . . . Torrence will be on duty tonight."

"Can I serve the soup?" Madame Maigret asked, sighing, shaking little bits of thread off her dress.

"Get my dinner jacket first. . . ."

As it was after eight, he dialed Galvani 47–53. It was the number of a young deputy. A maid answered, and he could hear the sound of knives and forks and an excited buzz of conversation.

"I'll go and call the magistrate. . . . Who is speaking? Superintendent Négret? . . ."

Through the open door of the bedroom, he could see the wardrobe and Madame Maigret taking out his dinner jacket.

"Is that you, Superintendent? . . . You don't speak English, do you? . . . Hello! Stay on the line. . . ." That's what I thought. . . . I wanted to say . . . it's about this case, naturally. . . . I think it would be better if you didn't get involved with . . . I mean not directly . . . with Mr. Clark and his staff. . . ."

There was a trace of a smile on Maigret's face.

"Monsieur Clark came to see me this afternoon with the governess. He's a man of some standing, with important connections. Before he came to see me, I had had a call from the American Embassy; they gave me a very favorable account of him. So you see what I mean? In a case like this, one must watch out not to make a mistake. . . .

"Monsieur Clark came with his lawyer and insisted on having his statement put on record.

"Hello! Are you listening, Superintendent?"

"Yes, sir. I'm listening. . . ."

The sound of forks in the background. The conversation had ceased. No doubt the deputy's guests were listening attentively to what the magistrate was saying.

"I'll put you briefly in the picture. Tomorrow morning my clerk can let you have the text of the statement. Monsieur Clark did have to go to Rome, then on to various other capitals, for business reasons. He had recently become engaged to Miss Ellen Darroman. . . ."

"Excuse me, sir. You said 'engaged'? I thought Monsieur Clark was married. . . ."

"Of course . . . That doesn't mean that he didn't intend to get divorced shortly. His wife didn't know yet. We can therefore say 'engaged.' He took advantage of the trip to Rome to . . ."

"To spend a night in Paris first with Miss Darroman . . ."

"Correct. But you're wrong, Superintendent, to indulge in sarcasm. Clark made an excellent impression on me. Morals aren't quite the same in his country as in ours, and divorce over there . . . Well, he made no secret of how he had spent the night. In your absence, I referred the matter to Inspector Ducuing for verification, to make doubly sure, but I'm certain Clark wasn't lying. Under the circumstances, it would be unfortunate if . . ."

Which meant, in fact:

"We are dealing with a man of the world, who has the protection of the American Embassy. So under the circumstances, don't interfere, because you're likely to be tactless and offend him. See the people in the basement, the maids, and so on. But leave Clark to me—I'll deal with him myself!"

"I understand, sir! Of course, sir . . ."

And, turning to his wife:

"You can serve the soup, Madame Maigret!"

It was nearly midnight. The long corridor at Police Headquarters was deserted, and so dimly lit that it seemed to be filled with a dense smog. Maigret's patent-leather shoes, which he seldom wore, creaked like those of a first-time communicant.

In his office, he began by raking up the stove and warming his hands, then, pipe in mouth, opened the door of the inspectors' office.

Ducuing was there, busy telling Torrence a story that they both seemed to find hilarious; anyway, they were in high spirits.

"Well, boys?"

And Maigret sat down on a corner of the ink-stained wooden table, tapping the ash from his pipe onto the floor. He could relax here, loosen his tie. The two inspectors had had beer sent up from the Brasserie Dauphine, and the Superintendent was pleased to see they hadn't forgotten him.

"You know, Chief, that man Clark's an odd fellow. . . . I went to have a good look at him in the Majestic bar, so that I could see him at close quarters and get a thorough impression. At that point I thought he looked like the typical businessman, a rather tough customer, in fact. . . . Well, now I know how he spent last night, and I can assure you he's quite a guy. . . ."

Torrence couldn't help eying the Superintendent's gleaming-white shirt front, adorned with two pearls, which he didn't often see him wearing.

"Listen. . . . First he and the girl dined in a cheap restaurant on Rue Lepic. . . . You know the kind I mean. The proprietor noticed them, because he doesn't often get asked for real champagne. Then they asked where they could find a merry-go-round. They had difficulty in explaining what they wanted. He finally directed them to the Foire du Trône.

"I caught up with them there. I don't know if they had a ride on the merry-go-round, but I imagine they did. They also had a go at the rifle range; I know, because Clark spent over a hundred francs there, much to the amazement of the good lady running it.

"You know the kind of thing . . . wandering through the crowd, arm in arm, like two young lovers. . . . But now we're coming to the best part. Listen. . . .

"You know Eugène the Muscle Man's booth? At the end of his show he challenged the crowd to have a try. There was a sort of colossus there who took up the challenge. Well . . . our Clark took him on. He went to get undressed behind a filthy canvas curtain and made short work of the giant. I imagine the girl was applauding in the front row of the crowd. Everyone was shouting.

" 'Atta boy, Englishman. . . . Bash his face in!'

"After which our two lovers went dancing at the Moulin de la Galette. And at about three they were to be seen at the Coupole, eating grilled sausages, and I imagine they then went quietly off to bed. . . .

"The Hotel Aiglon has no doorman. Only a night concierge, who sleeps in his little back room and pulls the rope without bothering too much about who comes in. He remembers hearing someone talking in English at about four in the morning. He says no one went out. . . .

"And that's it! Don't you think it's a pretty odd evening for people who are supposed to be staying at the Majestic?"

Maigret didn't answer one way or the other, and, glancing at his wristwatch, which he only wore on special occasions (it was a twentieth-wedding-anniversary present), got up from the table where he had been sitting.

"Good night, boys . . ."

He had reached the door, then turned back to finish his beer. He had to walk two or three hundred yards before he found a taxi.

"Rue Fontaine!"

It was 1:00 A.M. Night life in Montmartre was in full swing. A black doorman welcomed him to the Pélican, and he was obliged to leave his coat and hat in the cloakroom. On entering the main room, he hesitated a bit, as if unsure of himself; rolls of colored streamers were being tossed around.

"A table close to the floor show? . . . This way . . . Are you by yourself?"

41

He was reduced to muttering under his breath to the maître d'hôtel, who hadn't recognized him:

"Idiot!"

The barman, however, had spotted him at once, and was whispering to two hostesses who were propping themselves up at the bar.

Maigret sat down at a table, and as he couldn't drink beer here, he ordered a brandy and water. Less than ten minutes later the proprietor, who had been discreetly summoned, came to sit down opposite him.

"Nothing wrong, I hope, Superintendent? . . . You know I've always kept strictly within the law and . . ."

He glanced around the room, as if to check out what could have caused this unexpected visit from the police.

"Nothing . . ." Maigret replied. "I just felt like having a good time."

He pulled his pipe out of his pocket, but saw from the proprietor's face that it would be frowned upon here, and put it back with a sigh.

"If there's any information you need . . ." the other said, winking. "But I know all my staff personally. . . . I don't think there's anyone here at present who could be of interest to you. As for the customers, you can see for yourself. . . . The usual crowd . . . foreigners, people up from the provinces. Look! That man over there with Léa is a deputy. . . ."

Maigret got up and walked heavily over to the stairs that led to the washrooms. These were in a brightly lighted basement, with bluish tiles on the walls. There were telephone booths, mirrors, and a long table with numerous toilet articles: brushes, combs, a manicure set, every conceivable shade of powder, rouge, and so on.

"It's always the same when you dance with him. Give me another pair of stockings, Charlotte. . . ."

A plump young woman in an evening dress was sitting on a chair and had already taken off one stocking. She sat there with her skirt hitched up, inspecting her bare foot, while Charlotte rummaged in a drawer.

"Medium sheer, as usual?"

"Yes, that's fine, I'll take these. If a guy doesn't know how to dance, he ought at least . . ."

She caught sight of Maigret in the mirror and proceeded to put on her new stockings, glancing at him occasionally. Charlotte turned around; he saw her grow visibly paler when she noticed him.

"Ah! It's you. . . ."

She forced a laugh. She was no longer the same woman who had put her feet on the hob and who stuffed herself with pastries, in the little house in Saint-Cloud.

Her blonde hair was dressed with so much care that the waves seemed permanently glued in place. Her skin was a sugary pink. Her plump figure was sheathed in a very simple black silk dress, over which she wore a frilly little lace apron.

"Charge it with the rest, Charlotte."

"Will do."

The girl realized that the stranger was only waiting for her to leave, and as soon as she was back in her shoes, she hurried upstairs.

Charlotte, who was making a show of tidying the brushes and combs, was finally forced to ask:

"What do you want?"

Maigret didn't answer. He had sat down on the chair left vacant by the girl with the run in her stockings. As he was in the basement he seized the chance to fill his pipe, slowly, with immense care.

"If you think I know anything, you're mistaken. . . ."

It is a strange fact that women who have a placid disposition show their emotions the most. Charlotte was trying to stay calm, but she couldn't keep the waves of color from mounting to her face, or her hands from moving so clumsily over the toilet articles that she dropped a nail file.

"I could see, from the way you looked at me when you visited our house, that you thought . . ."

"I take it you never knew a dancer or night-club hostess called Mimi, is that correct?"

"That's correct."

"And yet you were a barmaid in Cannes for quite a long time . . . at the same time as this Mimi. . . ."

"There are lots of night clubs in Cannes, and you don't meet everyone, you know."

"You were at La Belle Etoile, weren't you?"

"What of it?"

"Nothing . . . I just wanted to come and have a chat with you. . . ."

They were silent for at least five minutes, because a customer came down, washed his hands, combed his hair, then asked for a cloth to polish his patent-leather shoes. When he had finally left a five-franc piece in the saucer and departed, the Superintendent continued:

"I like your Prosper Donge—I feel sure he's the nicest fellow in the world. . . ."

"That's a fact! You wouldn't believe how kind he is," she cried heatedly.

"He had a wretched childhood and everything has always been made so difficult for him."

44

"And do you know he never finished school, and everything he knows he's taught himself? If you look in his kitchen at the hotel you'll find books that people like us don't usually read. He's always had a passion for learning. . . . He's always dreamed of . . ."

Suddenly she stopped and tried to regain her composure.

"Did the telephone just ring?"

"No, I don't think so. . . ."

"What was I saying?"

"That he always dreamed of . . ."

"Oh, well! There's no secret about it. He would have liked to have a son, to make something of him. . . . Poor fellow, he got a raw deal with me, because ever since my operation I can't have children.

"Do you know Jean Ramuel?"

"No. I know he's the hotel bookkeeper and that he's in poor health, that's all. Prosper doesn't tell me much about the Majestic. Not like me; I tell him everything that happens here. . . ."

Having reassured her, he tried to make a bit of headway again.

"You see, what struck me was . . . I shouldn't tell you this . . . it's officially a secret. . . . But I feel sure it won't go any further. . . . Well, the automatic that was found in Mrs. Clark's handbag had been bought the day before at a gunsmith's on Faubourg Saint-Honoré. . . . Don't you think that that's very odd? There's this rich married woman, the mother of a family, who arrives from New York and stays in a luxury hotel on the Champs-Elysées, and who suddenly feels the need to buy a gun. . . . And note that it wasn't a pretty little lady's pistol, but a real weapon. . . ."

He avoided her eyes, looked at the gleaming toecaps of his shoes, as if amazed at how smart they were.

"Now we know that this same woman slipped down a back

45

staircase a few hours later, to get to the hotel basement. One is bound to think that she had a rendezvous, and to conclude that it was in view of this rendezvous that she had bought her gun. Suppose for a moment that this woman, who is now so respectable, had a wild past, and the someone who knew her then had tried to blackmail her. . . . Do you know if Ramuel ever lived on the Riviera? . . . Or a certain professional dancing partner called Zebio?"

"I don't know him."

He could tell, without looking at her, that she was on the point of bursting into tears.

"And there's one other person—the night concierge—who could have killed her, because he went down to the basement at about six in the morning. It was Prosper Donge who heard him going up the back stairs. Not to mention any of the *valets de chambre* . . . It's a great pity that you didn't know Mimi in Cannes. You could have given me details of all the people she knew then. . . . Oh well! I would much rather not have to go to Cannes, but I'm sure I'll find some of the people who knew her, down there. . . ."

He got up, tapped out his pipe, felt in his pocket for some change for the saucer.

"You don't need to do that!" she protested.

"Good night . . . I wonder what the train schedule is. . . ."

As soon as he got upstairs, he paid his bill and rushed to the bar across the street, a café frequented by employees from all the night clubs in the district.

"The telephone, please . . ."

He called the central exchange.

"This is the police speaking. Someone from the Pélican bar

will probably ask you for a Cannes number. Don't connect them too quickly. . . . Wait till I get to you."

He leaped into a taxi, rushed to the telephone exchange, and identified himself to the night supervisor.

"Give me some headphones. Have they put in a call for Cannes?"

"Yes, a minute ago . . . I found out whose number it is. . . . It's the Brasserie des Artistes, which stays open all night. Shall I put them through now?"

Maigret put on the headphones and waited. Some of the telephone girls, also wearing headphones, stared at him curiously.

"I'm connecting you with Cannes 18–43, mademoiselle. . . ."

"Thank you . . . Hello! The Brasserie des Artistes? . . . Who's speaking? . . . Is that you, Jean? . . . It's Charlotte here. . . . Yes? . . . Charlotte from La Belle Etoile . . . Wait . . . I'll shut the door. . . . I think there's someone . . ."

They heard her talking, probably to a customer. Then came the sound of a door being shut.

"Listen, Jean dear . . . it's very important. . . . I'll write and explain. . . . No, I'd better not—too risky. . . . I'll come and see you later, when it's all over. . . . Is Gigi still there? What? Still the same . . . Promise to tell her that if anyone questions her about Mimi . . . You remember? . . . Of course, you weren't there then. . . . Well, if she's asked anything at all about Mimi . . . she knows nothing! . . . And she must be particularly careful not to say anything about Prosper. . . ."

"Prosper who?" asked Jean at the other end of the line.

"Never mind. Just remember—she doesn't know anyone called Prosper, do you hear me? . . . Or Mimi . . . Hello! Are you there? . . . Is there someone else on the line? . . ."

Maigret realized that she was scared, that it had perhaps occurred to her that someone was listening to the conversation.

"You understand, Jean dear? . . . I can rely on you? . . . I'm hanging up because there's someone . . ."

Maigret also took off his headphones, and relighted his pipe, which had gone out.

"Did you learn what you wanted to know?" asked the supervisor.

"Yes, indeed. Get me the Gare de Lyon, train information. I need to know when there's a train for Cannes. . . . Provided I've got . . ."

He looked at his dinner jacket in irritation. Provided he had time to . . .

"Hello! . . . What did you say? . . . Seventeen minutes past four? . . . And I get there at two in the afternoon? . . . Thank you . . ."

Just time to rush to Boulevard Richard-Lenoir and to laugh at Madame Maigret's foul mood.

"Quick, my suit . . . a shirt . . . socks . . ."

At seventeen minutes past four he found himself on the Riviera Express, sitting opposite a woman who had a horrible Pekingese on her lap, and who kept looking sideways at Maigret, as though suspecting him of not liking dogs.

At about the same time, Charlotte was getting into a taxi, as she did every night. The driver dealt mostly with customers from the Pélican, and took her home free.

At five, Prosper Donge heard a car door slamming, the sound of the motor, footsteps, the key in the door.

But he didn't hear the usual "pfffttt" of the gas in the kitchen. Without pausing on the ground floor, Charlotte rushed upstairs and pushed the door open, panting:

48

"Prosper! . . . Listen! Don't pretend to be asleep. The Superintendent . . ."

Before she could explain, she had to undo her bra and take off her girdle, so that her stockings were left dangling around her legs.

"Look, it's serious! Well, get up then! . . . Do you think it's easy talking to a man who just lies there! . . ."

4

Gigi and the Carnival

For the next three hours, Maigret had the unpleasant feeling that he was floundering in a sort of no man's land between dream and reality. Perhaps it was his fault? Until just after Lyon, somewhere around Montélimar, the train was running through a tunnel of mist. The woman with the little dog, facing the Superintendent, didn't budge from her seat, and there were no empty compartments.

Maigret couldn't make himself comfortable. It was too hot. If he opened the window, it was too cold. So he went to the restaurant car and, to cheer himself up, drank whatever was available—coffee, then brandy, and then beer.

At about eleven, feeling sick, he told himself he'd feel better if he ate something, and ordered some ham and eggs, with no improvement forthcoming, however.

He was suffering from his sleepless night, the long hours on the train; he was in a very bad temper, in fact. After leaving Marseilles, he fell asleep in his corner, with his mouth open, then started awake, stupid with surprise, when he heard Cannes announced.

There was mimosa everywhere, under a brilliant Fourteenth of July sun. On the engines, on the coaches, on the station railings. And crowds of vacationers in light clothes, the men in white trousers . . .

Dozens of them were pouring out of a local train, wearing peaked caps, carrying brass instruments under their arms. He was hardly out of the station before he ran into another band, already rending the air with martial notes.

It was an orgy of light, sound, color, with flags and banners flying on all sides, and everywhere the golden-yellow mimosa, filling the whole town with its all-pervasive, sweetish scent.

"Excuse me, sergeant," he asked a festive-looking policeman, "can you tell me what it's all about?"

The man looked at him as though he had landed from the moon.

"Not heard of the Battle of Flowers?"

Other brass bands were winding through the streets, making for the sea, which could be glimpsed occasionally, pastel-blue, at the end of a street.

Later he remembered a little girl dressed as a pierrette, who was being dragged along hurriedly by her mother, probably so that they could get a good place for the pageant. This wouldn't have been so strange if the little girl hadn't been wearing an odd mask over her face, with a long nose, red cheeks, and drooping Chinese mustache. There she was, trotting along on her chubby little legs. . . .

He had no need to ask the way. As he walked down a quiet street toward the Croisette he saw a sign, BRASSERIE DES ARTISTES. And on a door beyond, the inscription HOTEL. He saw at a glance what kind of hotel it was.

He went in. Four men dressed in black, with rigid bow ties and white shirt fronts, were playing *belote*, filling time before they had to take their positions as croupiers in the casino. By the window, a girl was eating *choucroute garnie*. The waiter was wiping the tables. A young man, probably the proprietor, was reading a newspaper behind the bar. And from outside, from all directions, near and far, came echoes of the brass bands, and a stale whiff of mimosa, dust kicked up by the feet of the crowd, shouts, and the honking of horns. . . .

"A beer!" grunted Maigret, able at last to take off his heavy overcoat.

He found it almost embarrassing to be in the same dark colors as the croupiers.

He had exchanged glances with the proprietor as soon as he came in.

"Tell me, Monsieur Jean . . ."

And Monsieur Jean was clearly thinking:

"That one's probably a cop. . . ."

"How long have you owned this bar?"

"I took it over about three years ago. . . . Why?"

"And what did you do before that?"

"If it's of any interest to you, I was barman at the Café de la Paix, in Monte Carlo."

Only a hundred steps away, along the Croisette, were the luxury hotels: the Carlton, the Miramar, the Martinez, and others. . . .

It was clear that the Brasserie des Artistes was a background prop, as it were, to the more fashionable scene. The same was true of the whole street, with its dry cleaners, hairdressers, truck drivers' bistros, small businesses in the shadow of the grand hotels.

"The bar's open all night, isn't it?"

"That's right."

Not for the winter tourists, but for the casino and hotel staff, dancers, hostesses, bellboys, hotel touts, go-betweens of all kinds, pimps, tipsters, or night-club bouncers.

"Anything else you want to know?" Monsieur Jean asked curtly.

"I'd like you to tell me where I can find someone called Gigi. . . ."

"Gigi? Never heard of her . . ."

The woman eating *choucroute* was watching them wearily. The croupiers got up: it was nearly three o'clock.

"Look, Monsieur Jean . . . have you ever been in trouble over slot machines or anything like that?"

"What's that got to do with you?"

"I ask because if you've ever been convicted, the case will be much more serious. Charlotte's really good. She telephones her friends to ask their help, but forgets to tell them what it's about. So if one has a business like yours, if one's already been in trouble once or twice, one generally avoids becoming involved in anything criminal. Well—I'll telephone the Vice Squad, and I'm sure they won't have any difficulty telling me where I can find Gigi. Have you got a token?"

He got up and made a move toward the telephone booth.

"Excuse me! You spoke of becoming involved in a crime. . . . Is it serious?"

"Well, if a superintendent from Homicide comes down specially from Paris . . ."

"Just a minute, Superintendent . . . do you really want to see Gigi?"

"I've come more than a thousand kilometers to do so. . . ."

"All right, I'll take you to her. But I must warn you that she won't be able to tell you much. Do you know her? She's out of commission two days out of three. When she's got hold of some dope, if you see what I mean? Well, yesterday . . ."

"Yesterday, it so happened that after Charlotte's telephone call, she got hold of some, didn't she? Where is she?"

"This way . . . She's got a room somewhere in town, but last night she was incapable of walking."

A door led to the staircase of the hotel. The proprietor pointed to a room on the landing.

"Someone for you, Gigi!" he shouted.

And he waited at the top of the stairs until Maigret had shut the door. Then he went back to his counter, shrugged, and picked up his newspaper, looking a little worried despite himself.

The closed curtains let in only a luminous glow. The room was in a mess. A woman lay on the iron bed, with her clothes on, her hair disheveled, her face buried in the pillow. She began asking in a thick voice:

". . . d'you want?"

Then a very bleary eye appeared.

". . . been here before?"

Her nostrils were pinched, her complexion waxlike. Gigi was thin, angular, brown as a prune.

". . . time is it. Aren't you going to get undressed?"

She propped herself up on one elbow to drink some water and stared at Maigret, making a visible effort to pull herself together, and, seeing him sitting gravely on a chair by her bed, asked:

"You the doctor? . . ."

"What did Monsieur Jean tell you last night?"

"Jean . . . Jean's all right. . . . He gave me . . . But what's that got to do with you?"

"Yes, I know, he gave you some snow. . . . Lie down again. And he spoke to you about Mimi and Prosper."

57

The bands were still blaring outside, coming closer and then dying away, and the stale scent of mimosa persisted.

"Good old Prosper! . . ."

She spoke as if she were half asleep, her voice occasionally taking on a childish note. Then suddenly she screwed up her eyes, her forehead puckered as if she were in violent pain, and her mouth went slack.

"You've got some, haven't you?"

She was craving the drug. And Maigret had the distasteful sense of extracting secrets from a sick and delirious person.

"You were fond of Prosper, weren't you?"

"He's not like other people. . . . He's too good. . . . He shouldn't have fallen for a woman like Mimi, but that's always the way. . . . Do you know him?"

Come on now! Pull yourself together. Wasn't that what he, Maigret, had come for?

"That was when he was at the Miramar, wasn't it? . . . There were three of you dancing at La Belle Etoile, Mimi, Charlotte, and you. . . ."

She stuttered solemnly:

"You mustn't say unkind things about Charlotte, she's a good girl. . . . And she was in love with Prosper. If he'd listened to me . . ."

"I suppose you met at the café, after work. . . . Prosper was Mimi's lover. . . ."

"He was so much in love with her it made him idiotic. . . . Poor Prosper! . . . And afterward, when she . . ."

She sat up suddenly, suspicious.

"Are you really a friend of his?"

"When she had a baby, you mean? . . ."

"Who told you that? I was the only person she wrote to about it. . . . But it didn't start like that. . . ."

She was listening to the music, which was again coming closer.

"What's that?"

"Nothing . . ."

The flower-decked floats were filing along the Croisette as guns were fired to announce the start. Blazing sun, calm sea, motorboats cutting circles through the water, and small yachts gracefully swooping . . .

"You're sure you haven't got the stuff? Won't you go and get some from Jean?"

"It all started when she left with the American?"

"Did Prosper tell you that? . . . Give me another glass of water, will you? Thanks. A Yank she met at La Belle Etoile, who fell in love with her. He took her to Deauville and then to Biarritz. Mimi knew how to handle herself, she had style. . . . She wasn't like the rest of us. Is Charlotte still working at the Pélican? And look at me!"

She gave a ghastly laugh, disclosing teeth in wretched condition.

"One day, she wrote that she was going to have a baby and that she would make the American believe it was his. What was he called again? Oswald. Then she wrote to tell me that it nearly didn't work because the baby had carrot-colored hair. Think of it! I wouldn't want Prosper to know that."

Was it the effect of the two glasses of water? She pulled one leg after the other out of bed, long, thin legs that would attract few male glances. Standing, she appeared tall, skeletal. What long hours she must spend pacing up and down the dark sidewalk or loitering at a café table before she found any takers.

Her stare became more fixed. She examined Maigret from head to toe.

"You're from the police, aren't you?"

She was getting angry. But her mind was still hazy and she had to make an effort to clear her thoughts.

"What was it Jean told me? Ah, yes . . . And who brought you here, anyway? He made me promise to keep my mouth shut. Say it—say that you're from the police! And I . . . What's it to the police if Prosper and Mimi . . ."

The storm broke, suddenly, violently, sickeningly: "You filthy bastard! Dirty swine! You saw the state I'm in and you . . ."

She had opened the door, and the sounds from outside could be heard even more clearly.

"Get out of here or . . ."

It was ridiculous, pathetic. Maigret just managed to sidestep the jug she threw at his legs, and she was still screaming after him as he went down the stairs.

The bar was empty. It was too early for customers.

"Well?" Monsieur Jean asked, from behind his counter.

Maigret put on his coat and hat and left a tip for the waiter.

"Did she come through?"

A voice sounded from the stairs:

"Jean! . . . Jean! . . . Come here—I must tell you . . ."

It was poor wretched Gigi, who had padded down in her stockings and now pushed a disheveled head in through the doorway of the bar.

Maigret thought it better to leave.

On the Croisette, in his black coat and bowler hat, he must have looked like a tourist from the provinces come to see the carnival on the Riviera for the first time. Masked figures bumped into him. He had difficulty disentangling himself from the brass bands. On the beach, a few winter visitors were ignoring the festival and sunbathing, their almost naked bodies already brown, covered with oil.

The Miramar was down there, a vast yellow structure with two or three hundred windows, with its doorman, car attendants, and touts. He nearly went in, but what was the use?

Didn't he already know everything he needed to know? He could no longer tell whether he was thirsty or drunk. He went into a bar.

"Do you have the train schedule?"

"To Paris? There's an express—first, second, and third class—at eight-forty."

He had another beer. There were hours to go. He couldn't think what to do. Later, he was to have nightmarish memories of those empty hours spent in Cannes, surrounded by carnival noises.

At times, the past became so real to him that he could literally see Prosper, with his red hair, big, candid eyes, pock-marked skin, coming out of the Miramar by the little back door and hurrying across to the Brasserie des Artistes.

The three women, six years younger at the time, would be there having lunch or dinner. Prosper was ugly—he knew it—and he was passionately in love with Mimi, the youngest and prettiest of the three.

His pleading eyes must have made them laugh, cruelly, at first.

"Don't, Mimi," Charlotte might have said. "He's a sweetheart. You never know what may come of it. . . ."

Then La Belle Etoile, in the evening. Prosper never set foot inside. He knew his place. But he met them in the early morning, to eat onion soup at the café.

"If a man like that loved me, I would . . ."

Charlotte must have been impressed by his humble devotion. And Gigi wasn't yet on cocaine.

"Don't pay attention, Monsieur Prosper! She pretends to make fun of you, but actually . . ."

They had become lovers, had lived together, perhaps. Prosper

61

must have spent most of his savings on presents. Until an American tourist . . .

Had Charlotte told him, later, that the child was definitely his?

Kind, generous Charlotte—she knew he didn't love her, that he still loved Mimi, and yet she was living with him, contentedly, in their little house in Saint-Cloud.

While Gigi slipped further and further . . .

"Some flowers, monsieur? To send to your girl friend . . ."

The flower seller spoke ironically, because Maigret didn't look like a man who has a girl friend. But he sent a basket of mimosa to Madame Maigret. Then, as he still had half an hour before train time, a hunch made him telephone Paris. He was in a small bar near the station. Dust spotted the trousers of the musicians from the bands. Whole carloads of them were leaving for nearby stations, and the fine Sunday afternoon was drawing drowsily to a close.

"Hello! Is that you, Chief? You're still in Cannes?"

He could tell from Lucas's voice that he was excited.

"Things have been humming here. The examining magistrate is furious. He's just telephoned to know what you are doing. Hello? They made the discovery only three quarters of an hour ago. It was Torrence, who was on duty at the Majestic, who telephoned. . . ."

Maigret stood listening in the narrow booth, and grunted from time to time. Through the window, he could see, in the light from the setting sun that filled the bar, the musicians in their white linen trousers and silver-braided caps, and now and then one of them would jokingly sound a long note on his bombardon or trombone, while the golden liquid sparkled in the glasses.

"Right! . . . I'll be there tomorrow morning. . . . No! Of course . . . Well, if the magistrate insists, you'll have to arrest him."

It had only just happened, then. Downstairs at the Majestic . . . Tea-dance time, with music drifting along the passageways. Prosper Donge like a great goldfish in his glass cage . . . Jean Ramuel, yellow as a quince, in his . . .

From what Lucas said—but the inquiry had not yet started—the night concierge had been seen wandering in the corridors, without his uniform, in his own clothes. No one knew what he was doing there. People were too busy with their own affairs to bother about such details.

The night concierge, Justin Colleboeuf, was a quiet, dull little man who spent the night alone in the lobby. He didn't read. There was no one to talk to. And he didn't go to sleep, either. He just sat there, on a chair, hour after hour, staring straight ahead of him.

His wife was the concierge at a new apartment house in Neuilly.

What was Colleboeuf doing in the hotel at half past four in the afternoon?

Zebio, the dancer, had gone to the cloakroom to put on his dinner jacket.

Everyone was going about his business. Ramuel had come out of his booth several times.

At five o'clock, Prosper Donge had gone to the cloakroom. He took off his white jacket and put on his own jacket and coat, and collected his bicycle.

Then, a few minutes later, a bellboy went into the cloakroom. He noticed that the door to locker 89 was slightly open. The next minute the whole hotel was alerted by his yells.

In the locker, bent over, in a gray overcoat, was the body of the night concierge. His felt hat was at the back of the locker.

Like Mrs. Clark, Justin Colleboeuf had been strangled. The body was still warm.

Meanwhile, Prosper Donge, on his bike, peacefully crossed

the Bois de Boulogne, went over the Pont de Saint-Cloud, and got off his bicycle to walk up the steep road to his house.

"A pastis!" Maigret ordered, as there didn't seem to be anything else on the counter.

Then he got into the train, his head as heavy as it had been when, as a child, he had spent a long day in the country, in the blazing sun.

5

Spit on the Window

They had been traveling for some time. Maigret had already taken off his jacket, tie, and stiff collar, as the compartment was once again too hot; it was as though hot air, and the smell of the train, were oozing from everywhere—woodwork, floor, seats.

He bent over to unlace his shoes. Not content with his free first-class pass, he had taken a sleeper; too bad if anyone at home objected. And the guard had promised him that he would have his compartment to himself.

Suddenly, as he was still bending over his shoes, he had the unpleasant feeling that someone was looking at him, from close by. He looked up. There was a pale face peering through the window from the corridor. Dark eyes, a large mouth badly made up or, rather, enlarged, by two streaks of red applied at random, which had then run.

But the most noticeable thing about the face was its expression of dislike, of hatred. How had Gigi got herself there? Before Maigret could put on his shoe again, the girl's face puckered in disgust and she spat on the window, in his direction, then went back down the corridor.

He remained impassive and got dressed. Before leaving the compartment, he lighted a pipe, as if for moral support. Then he went down the corridor, from car to car, assiduously looking into each compartment. The train was a long one. Maigret walked through at least ten coaches, bumped into the partitions, had to disturb fifty or more people.

"Sorry . . . sorry . . ."

He came to the point where the carpet ended and the third-class compartments began. People were dozing six to a side. Others were eating. Children stared into space.

In a compartment with two sailors from Toulon who were going "up" to Paris, and an old couple who were nodding off, mouths agape, the woman clutching her basket on her lap, he found Gigi, huddled in a corner.

He hadn't noticed earlier, in the corridor, how she was dressed. He had been so surprised that he had only taken in that it wasn't the Gigi of the Brasserie des Artistes, with her wandering gaze and slack mouth.

Wrapped in a cheap fur coat, her legs crossed to reveal down-at-heel shoes and a large run in her stocking, she stared straight ahead of her. Had she succeeded, on her own, in dragging herself out of the comatose state in which she had been that afternoon? Had someone given her something to wake her up? Or possibly had a new dose of cocaine revived her?

She became aware of Maigret standing in the corridor but made no move. He watched her for a while, trying to signal to her; she still took no notice. So he opened the door.

"Would you come out for a minute?"

She hesitated. The two sailors were staring at her. Make a scene? She shrugged and got up to join him, and he shut the door.

"Haven't you done enough?" she hissed at him. "You should be pleased with yourself, shouldn't you? You should feel proud of yourself! You took advantage of the mess I was in. . . ."

He saw that she was about to cry, that her garishly painted mouth was trembling, and turned away.

"And you didn't lose any time in locking him up, did you!"

"Tell me, Gigi. How do you know Prosper has been arrested?"

A weary gesture.

"Haven't you heard? I thought the wire-tapping would see to that. It doesn't matter if I tell you, because you'll soon know anyway. Charlotte telephoned Jean. Prosper had just got back from work when a taxi full of cops arrived and took him away. Charlotte's in a terrible state. She wanted to know if I'd talked. And I did talk, didn't I? I told you enough to . . ."

A violent jolt of the train made her fall against Maigret, and she recoiled in horror.

"You won't send him up, not if I can help it! Even if Prosper did kill that dirty bitch Mimi . . . I'll tell you something, Superintendent. . . . On my honor, the honor of a prostitute, a slut who has nothing to lose, I swear to you that if he's condemned to death, I'll find you and plug you full of holes."

She paused for a moment, scornfully. He didn't say anything. He felt it wasn't an empty threat, that she was just the type, in fact, to wait for him on some lonely street corner and empty her automatic into him.

The two sailors were still watching them from the compartment.

"Good night," he sighed.

He went back to his sleeper, got undressed at last, and lay down.

The dimmed light was shedding a vague blue glow on the ceiling. Maigret lay there with his eyes shut, frowning.

One question kept worrying him. Why had the examining magistrate ordered Prosper Donge's arrest? What had the magistrate, who had not left Paris and who did not know Gigi, or the Brasserie des Artistes, ferreted out? Why arrest Donge, rather than Jean Ramuel or Zebio?

He felt vaguely apprehensive. He knew the magistrate.

Maigret hadn't said anything when he saw him arrive at the Majestic with the public prosecutor, but he had made a face, because he had worked with him in the past.

He was a man of integrity, certainly, a good family man even, who collected rare editions. He had a fine, square-cut gray beard. Maigret had once accompanied him on a raid of a gambling house. It was in the daytime, when the place was empty. Pointing to the large baccarat tables shrouded under dust covers, the magistrate had asked ingenuously:

"Are those billiard tables?"

Then, with that same innocence of a man who has never set foot in a low dive, he had been amazed to discover three exits into three different streets, one of them leading, via the basement, to another building. He was even more astonished to learn from the account books that certain players were given large advances, because he didn't know that in order to make people play, you have first to get them hooked.

Why had the magistrate, whose name was Bonneau, suddenly decided to have Donge arrested?

Maigret slept badly, waking up each time the train stopped, and the noise and jolting of the carriages became mixed with his nightmares.

When he got off the train at the Gare de Lyon, it was still dark, and a fine, cold rain was falling. Lucas was there, with his coat collar turned up, stamping his feet to keep himself warm.

"Not too tired, Chief?"

"Have you got someone with you?"

"No. If you need another officer, I saw one of our men in the waiting room."

"Go and get him."

Gigi got out, shook hands with the two sailors in a friendly good-by, and shrugged as she went past the Superintendent. She had gone a few steps when she suddenly turned back.

"You can have me followed if you want. I can tell you in advance that I'm going to see Charlotte."

Lucas came back.

"I couldn't find the man."

"Never mind. Come along."

They took a taxi.

"Now, tell me what's happened. Why has the magistrate . . ."

"I was going to tell you. He summoned me just after the second crime had been committed and he had sent some men to arrest Donge. He asked me if we had any news, if you'd telephoned, and so on. Then he handed me a letter, with a nasty smile. An anonymous letter . . . I can't remember the exact words. It said that Mrs. Clark, who was once a chorus girl called Mimi, had been Donge's mistress, that she had a child by him, and that he had often threatened her. You look as though you're upset, Chief."

"Go on. . . ."

"That's all. . . . The magistrate was delighted.

"So, you see, it's an open-and-shut case!" he concluded. "Ordinary blackmail . . . And as Mrs. Clark no doubt didn't want to pay up . . . I'll go and interrogate Donge shortly in his cell.''

''He's there already?''

But the taxi had pulled up at the Quai des Orfèvres. It was half past five in the morning. A thick yellow mist rose from the Seine. Maigret slammed the car door.

''He's at the station? . . . Come with me. . . .''

They had to go around the Palais de Justice to get to the Quai de l'Horloge; they went on foot, without hurrying.

''Yes. The magistrate telephoned me again at about nine last night to say that Donge had refused to speak. It appears that he said he would talk only to you. . . .''

''Did you get any sleep last night?''

''Two hours, on a sofa.''

''Go and get some rest. Be at Headquarters at about noon.''

And Maigret went into the Central Police Station. A police van was coming out. There had been a raid at the Bastille, and about thirty women had been brought in, some of them newcomers, without identity cards. They sat in cubicles around the vast, badly lighted room. There was a barracks-room smell, and the air was thick with raucous voices and obscene jokes.

''Where is Donge? Is he asleep?''

''He hasn't slept a wink. You'll see for yourself.''

The separate cells were shut by doors with bars, as in a stable. In one of them a man with his head in his hands was sitting, a barely discernible figure silhouetted against the darkness.

The key turned in the lock. The hinges creaked. The tall, drooping man got up, as though coming out of a dream. His tie and shoelaces had been taken away. His red hair was unkempt.

''It's you, Superintendent . . .'' he whispered.

And he rubbed his eyes with his hand, as if to make sure that it was really Maigret.

72

"I hear you wanted to speak with me?"

"I thought it would be best. . . ."

And he asked, with childish innocence:

"The magistrate isn't cross? What could I have told him? He was so sure I was guilty. He even showed my hands to his clerk, saying they were a strangler's hands."

"Come with me. . . ."

Maigret hesitated a moment. What was the point of putting handcuffs on him? They must have done so to bring him to the station: the marks were still on his wrists.

They went in single file along dark corridors, which had little in common with those in the Majestic basement. Running under the vast Palais de Justice, they connected with Police Headquarters, where they suddenly emerged in a brightly lighted passageway.

"In here . . . Have you had anything to eat?"

The other indicated that he hadn't. Maigret, who was also hungry, and thirsty, too, sent the man on duty to get beer and sandwiches.

"Sit down, Donge. Gigi is in Paris. She must be with Charlotte by now. Cigarette?"

He didn't smoke, but he always kept cigarettes in his drawer. Prosper lighted one clumsily, as if, in the space of a few hours, he had lost all his self-assurance. He was troubled by his gaping shoes, the absence of a tie, and the smell that, after only one night in the cells, emanated from his clothes.

Maigret stirred up the fire. All the other offices had central heating, which he loathed, and he had managed to keep the old iron stove that had been there for twenty years.

"Sit down. . . . They're bringing us something to eat. . . ."

Donge was hesitating about whether to tell him something,

and, when he finally decided to speak, stammered in an anguished voice:

"Did you see the little boy?"

"No."

"I saw him for a moment in the hotel lobby. I can swear to you, Superintendent, he's . . ."

"Your son. I know."

"You should see him! His hair's as red as mine. He has my hands, my large bones. They used to laugh at me, when I was a child, because of my big bones."

The beer and sandwiches arrived. Maigret ate standing up, pacing back and forth in his office, while outside the sky over Paris began to grow lighter.

"I can't . . ." Donge finally sighed, timidly putting his sandwich back on the plate. "I'm not hungry. Whatever happens, they won't take me back at the Majestic now, or anywhere else. . . ."

His voice shook. He was waiting for Maigret to help him, but the Superintendent let him flounder on.

"Do you think I killed her, too?"

As Maigret didn't answer, he nodded miserably. He wanted to explain it all now, persuade his interrogator; but he didn't know where to begin.

"You see, I never had much to do with women. In our trade . . . And always working down in the basement . . . Some of them burst out laughing when I showed I was fond of them. With a face like mine, you see . . . Then, when I knew Mimi, at the Brasserie des Artistes . . . There were three of them. . . . You know about that. And it's odd how it's turned out, isn't it? If I had chosen one of the other two . . . But no! I had to fall in love with *her*! Crazily in love, Superintendent . . . madly in love! She could have done anything she liked with me!

74

And I thought she'd agree to marry me one day. Well, do you know what the magistrate said to me last night? I can't remember what he said, exactly. . . . It made me sick. He said that what I had really been after was the money she brought in. He took me for a . . ."

Maigret looked out of the window to spare him further embarrassment, watching the Seine turn to a pale silver.

"She left with this American. I hoped that he'd desert her when he got back to America and that she'd come back to me. Then one day we heard that he'd married her. The news made me ill. It was Charlotte who, out of the kindness of her heart, looked after me. I told her I couldn't live in Cannes any longer. Every street brought back memories. I looked for a job in Paris. Charlotte offered to come with me. And you may find it hard to believe, but for a long time we lived together as brother and sister."

"Did you know that Mimi had had a child?" Maigret asked, emptying his pipe into the coal bucket.

"All I knew was that she was living somewhere in America. It was only when Charlotte thought I had got over it . . . In time, you see, we had become a real couple. One evening, a neighbor burst into our house; he was beside himself. His wife was about to have a baby, much earlier than had been expected. He was frantic. He asked us to help. Charlotte went over. The next day, she said to me:

" 'Poor old Prosper . . . What a state you would have been in, if . . .'

"And then, I don't know quite how it happened . . . bit by bit, she told me that Mimi had a child. Mimi had written to Gigi to tell her. She had explained that she had used the child to make him marry her, though it was definitely mine. . . .

"I went to Cannes. Gigi showed me the letter, because she'd kept it, but she refused to give it to me, and I think she burned it.

"I wrote to America. I begged Mimi to give me my son, or at the very least to send me a photograph of him. She didn't answer. I didn't even know if it was the right address.

"And I kept thinking:

"Now my son will be doing this . . . now he's doing that. . . ."

He was silent, choking with emotion, and Maigret pretended to be busy sharpening a pencil, while doors began to bang in the corridors.

"Did Charlotte know you'd written?"

"No. I wrote the letter at the hotel. Three years passed. One day I was looking at some of the foreign magazines guests leave on their tables. I got a shock seeing a photograph of Mimi with a little boy of five. It was a newspaper from Detroit, Michigan, and the caption said something like: 'The elegant Mrs. Oswald J. Clark and her son, who have just returned from a cruise in the Pacific.'

"I wrote again."

"What did you write?" Maigret asked, in an even tone.

"I don't remember. I was going mad. I begged her to reply. I said . . . I think I said I'd come over, that I'd tell everyone the truth, or that if she refused to give me my son, I'd . . ."

"Yes?"

"I swear I wouldn't have done it. Yes, I may have threatened to kill her. . . . When I think that for a week she was living over my head, with the boy, and that I never suspected. . . .

"I only discovered by chance. . . . You saw the personnel dining room. Names don't exist for us, down in the basement. We know that Room 117 has chocolate in the morning and that

Room 452 has bacon and eggs. We know the maid from Room 123 and the chauffeur from Room 216.

"It was silly. I went into the personnel dining room. I heard a woman speaking to a chauffeur in English, and she mentioned the name Mrs. Clark.

"As I don't speak English, I got the bookkeeper to ask her. He asked her if she was talking about a Mrs. Clark from Detroit, and if she had her son with her. . . .

"When I learned they were there, I tried, for a whole day, to catch sight of them, either in the lobby or in the corridor on their floor. But it's difficult for us to go where we want. I didn't succeed.

"Don't get me wrong. I don't know if you'll understand. . . . If Mimi had asked to come and live with me again, I couldn't have. . . . Have I stopped loving her? That may be it. I only know that I wouldn't have the heart to leave Charlotte, who's been so kind to me.

"Well, I didn't want to upset things for her. I wanted her to find a way to give me back my son. I know Charlotte would be only too happy to bring him up."

Maigret looked at him at that moment, and was struck by the intensity of Prosper Donge's emotion. If he hadn't known Donge had only had one beer—and had not even finished that—he would have thought he was drunk. The blood had rushed to his face. His eyes shone—large, protruding eyes. He wasn't crying, but he drew huge, sobbing breaths.

"Have you got any children, sir?"

It was Maigret's turn to feel embarrassed; Madame Maigret's great sorrow was that they had no children. It was something he tried not to talk about.

"The magistrate talked all the time. According to him, I had

77

done all kinds of things, for all sorts of reasons. But it wasn't like that at all. Having spent every spare moment of the entire day prowling along the hotel corridors, in the vain hope of seeing my son, I no longer knew what I was doing. And the telephone ringing all the time, and the dumbwaiters, and my three assistants, and the coffeepots and creamers to fill . . . I sat down in a corner. . . ."

"In the breakfast kitchen, you mean?"

"That's right. I wrote a letter. . . . I wanted to see Mimi. . . . I remembered that at six o'clock in the morning I was nearly always alone downstairs. I begged her to come."

"You didn't threaten her?"

"Possibly, at the end of the letter. Yes, I must have written that if she didn't come within three days, I would do what I had to. . . ."

"And what did you mean by 'what you had to'?"

"I don't know. . . ."

"Would you have killed her?"

"I couldn't have done it."

"You would have kidnapped the child?"

He gave a pathetic, almost half-witted smile.

"Do you think I could have done it?"

"Would you have told her husband everything?"

Prosper Donge's eyes opened wide in horror.

"No! I swear to you! . . . I think . . . Yes, I think that if it had come to the worst, I would have killed her in a moment of anger, rather than do that. But that morning, I had a flat tire at Avenue Foch. I got to the Majestic nearly a quarter of an hour late. I didn't see Mimi. I thought that she had come, and when she couldn't find me, had gone back to her suite. If I had known her husband had left, I would have gone up by the back stairs. But there again, we in the basement know nothing about what's going

78

on above our heads. I was worried. That morning, I can't have seemed myself. . . ."

Maigret suddenly interrupted him.

"What made you go and open locker 89?"

"I can tell you why. And it proves I'm not lying, at any rate to anyone from the police, because if I'd known she was dead, I wouldn't have acted as I did. It was about a quarter to nine when the waiter on the second floor sent down the order for Suite 203. On the slip there was—you can check this, because the management keeps them—there was: one hot chocolate, one bacon and eggs, and one tea."

"Which meant?"

"I'll explain. I knew that the chocolate was for the boy, the bacon and eggs for the nurse. . . . So there were only two of them there. Every other day at that time there was an order for black coffee and toast for Mimi. So, I put the black coffee and toast on the tray, too. I sent the dumbwaiter up. A few minutes later the coffee and toast were sent back. It may seem odd to you to have attached so much importance to these details. But don't forget that in the basement that's about all we see of what people are doing.

"I went to the telephone.

" 'Hello! Didn't Mrs. Clark want her breakfast?'

" 'Mrs. Clark isn't in her room.'

"Please believe me, Superintendent. . . . The magistrate didn't believe me. . . . I was certain that something had happened."

"What did you think had happened?"

"Oh, well! . . . I thought of the husband. I thought that if he had followed her . . ."

"Who took the letter up for you?"

"A bellboy. He assured me he had given it to the right person.

But those boys lie as soon as breathe. It comes from being with such an odd bunch of people. And then Clark might have found the letter. . . .

"So—I don't know if anyone saw me, but I opened nearly all the doors in the basement. Of course, no one takes much notice of anyone else, so perhaps no one noticed me. I went into the cloakroom. . . ."

"Was the door of locker 89 really open?"

"No. I opened all the empty lockers. Do you believe me? Will anyone believe me? No, they won't, will they? And that's why I didn't tell the truth. I was waiting. I hoped no one would pay any attention to me. It was only when I saw that I was the only one you weren't questioning . . . I've never felt so awful as I did that day, while you walked up and down in the basement without saying a single word to me, without seeming to see me! I didn't know what I was doing. I forgot the installment I had to go and pay. I had to turn back again. Then you joined me in the Bois de Boulogne and I knew you were on my track. . . .

"The next morning, Charlotte said when she woke me up:

" 'Why didn't you tell me you had killed her?' "

"So you see, if even Charlotte . . ."

It had become broad daylight, and Maigret hadn't noticed. A stream of buses, taxis, and delivery trucks was crossing the bridge. Paris had come to life again.

Then, after a long silence, and in an even more miserable voice, Prosper Donge mumbled:

"The boy doesn't even speak French! I asked. . . . You couldn't go and see him, Superintendent?"

And suddenly frantic:

"You're not going to let him go away again?"

"Hello! . . . Superintendent Maigret? . . . The boss's asking for you. . . . "

Maigret sighed and left his office. It was time to make his report.

He was in the director's office for twenty minutes. When he got back, Donge was sitting there unmoving, leaning forward with his arms crossed on the table and his head resting on his arms.

The Superintendent was worried in spite of himself. But when he touched the prisoner's arm, he slowly looked up, with no attempt to hide his pockmarked face, which was wet with tears.

"The magistrate wants to question you again in his office. I advise you to repeat exactly what you have told me."

An inspector was waiting at the door.

"Forgive me if . . ."

Maigret took a pair of handcuffs from his pocket, and there was a double click.

"It's the regulation!" he sighed.

Then, alone in his office once more, he opened the window and breathed in the damp air. It was a good ten minutes before he went into the inspectors' office.

He appeared fresh and rested again and asked in his usual way:

"Ready, boys?"

6

Charlotte's Letter

Two policemen were sitting on the bench, leaning against the wall, their arms crossed on their chests, and their booted legs stretched out as far as possible, barring the way down the hall.

A low murmur of voices came through the door beside them. All along the hallway were other doors flanked by benches, on most of which sat policemen, some with a handcuffed prisoner between them.

It was noon. Maigret was smoking his pipe, waiting to be asked into Examining Magistrate Bonneau's office.

"What's in there?" he asked one of the policemen, pointing to the door.

The reply was as laconic and as eloquent as the question: "Jeweler from Rue Saint-Martin."

A girl, slumped on the bench, was staring despairingly at the door of another magistrate. She blew her nose, wiped her eyes, and twisted her hands, tugging at her fingers in a paroxysm of anxiety.

The grim sounds of Monsieur Bonneau's voice grew more distinct. The door opened. Maigret automatically stuffed his pipe, which was still warm, into his pocket. The boy who came out, and who was at once seized by the policemen, had the insolent air of a hard-core delinquent. He turned around to say to the magistrate, with biting sarcasm:

"I'll be delighted to come and see you any time you say, sir!"

He saw Maigret and frowned; then, as if reassured, winked at the Superintendent. The latter's face, at that moment, had the abstracted look of someone who vaguely remembers something without quite knowing what it is.

He heard, from behind the door, which had been left open:

"Ask the Superintendent to come in. You can go now, Monsieur Benoit, I won't need you any more this morning."

Maigret went in, still searching his memory. What was it that had struck him about the prisoner who had just left the magistrate's office?

"Good morning, Superintendent. Not too tired, I hope? Please sit down. I don't see your pipe. You may smoke. Well, how was your trip to Cannes?"

Monsieur Bonneau wasn't a spiteful man, but he was obviously delighted to have succeeded where the police had failed. He tried unsuccessfully to hide the gleam of satisfaction in his eye.

"It's funny that we both discovered the same things, I in Paris, without leaving my office, and you on the Riviera . . . don't you think?"

"Very funny, yes . . ."

Maigret had the polite smile of a guest who is forced by his hostess to have a second helping of a dish he detests.

"Well, what are your conclusions on the affair, Superintendent? This Prosper Donge? I have his statement here. It seems he merely repeated to me what he'd already told you this morning. He admits everything, in fact. . . ."

"Except the two crimes," Maigret said quietly.

"Except the two crimes, naturally! That would be too good to be true! He admits that he threatened his ex-mistress; he admits that he asked her to meet him at six in the morning in the basement of the hotel, and his letter can't have been very reassuring because the poor woman went straight out to buy a gun. Then he tells us this story of the flat tire that made him late."

"It isn't a story. . . ."

"How do you know? He could easily have made a puncture in his tire when he got to the hotel."

"But he didn't. I've found the policeman who called out to him about his tire that morning, at the corner of Avenue Foch."

"It's only a detail, anyway," said the magistrate hurriedly, not wanting to have his beautiful reconstruction undermined. "Tell me, Superintendent, have you looked into Donge's past history?"

The glint of satisfaction was again clearly visible in Monsieur Bonneau's eye, and he couldn't help stroking his beard in anticipation.

"I dare say you haven't had time. I made a point of consulting the records. I was given his dossier, and I discovered that our man, so docile in appearance, is not a first offender."

Maigret was forced to look contrite.

"It's strange," the magistrate went on, "we have these records right above us, on the top floor of the Palais de Justice, and we so often forget to consult them! . . . Well, we find Prosper Donge, at the age of sixteen, with a job as a dishwasher in a café in Vitry-le-François, stealing fifty francs from the till, running away, and being caught in a train en route to Lyon. He promises

87

to reform, of course. He narrowly escapes being sent to a correctional institute and is put on probation for two years."

The odd thing was that while the magistrate was carrying on, Maigret kept thinking:

"Where the devil did I see . . . ?"

And he wasn't thinking of Donge, but of the boy who had come out as he went in.

"Fifteen years later, in Cannes, three months suspended sentence for criminal assault and insulting behavior to a policeman . . . And now, Superintendent, perhaps it's time I showed you something. . . ."

He held out a small paper square of the kind sold in old-fashioned stationery shops or used as checks in small cafés. The text was written in violet ink, with a leaky pen, and the writing was that of an ill-educated woman.

It was the anonymous letter that had been sent to the magistrate, informing him of Prosper and Mimi's affair.

"Here is the envelope. As you see, it was dropped between midnight and six in the morning into the mailbox on Place Clichy. Place Clichy, mind you. Now, take a look at this notebook. . . ."

A rather grubby school notebook, covered with grease marks, it contained recipes—some cut from newspapers and stuck in, others copied out.

This time, Maigret frowned, and the magistrate couldn't disguise a triumphant smile.

"You would agree that it's the same writing? I felt sure you would. . . . Well, Superintendent, this notebook was taken from the dresser in a kitchen that you already know, in Saint-Cloud—at Prosper Donge's house, in fact—and these recipes were copied out by a certain Charlotte. . . . "

He was so pleased with himself that he made a show of apologizing.

"I know you police and our department don't always see things in quite the same light. At the Quai des Orfèvres, you have a certain sympathy for a particular kind of person, for certain irregular situations, which we as magistrates have difficulty in sharing. Admit, Superintendent, it is not always we who are wrong. And tell me why, if this Prosper is the upright man he appears, his own mistress, this Charlotte, who also pretends to be so kindhearted, should send me an anonymous letter to destroy him?"

"I don't know. . . ."

Maigret seemed staggered.

"This case can be wound up pretty quickly now. I've sent Donge to the Santé prison. When you've interrogated the woman, Charlotte . . . As for the second crime, it can easily be explained. The poor night concierge . . . Colleboeuf, I believe? . . . must have been party to the first crime. At any rate he knew who Mrs. Clark's murderer was. He couldn't rest all day. And finally, no doubt, tortured by indecision, he came back to the Majestic to warn the murderer that he was going to denounce him. . . ."

The telephone rang.

"Hello! Yes . . . I'm on my way. . . ."

And to Maigret:

"It's my wife, to remind me that we have some friends coming for lunch. I will leave you to your inquiry, Superintendent. I think you now have enough leads to . . ."

Maigret was almost at the door when he turned back, with the look of someone who has at last pinned down what he had been trying to remember for some time.

"About Fred, sir . . . It *was* Fred-the-Marseillais you were interrogating when I arrived, wasn't it?"

"It's the sixth time I've interrogated him without discovering the names of his accomplices."

"I met Fred about three weeks ago, at Angelino's, on Place d'Italie. . . ."

The magistrate stared at him, clearly unable to see the relevance of this remark.

"Angelino, who has a 'club' frequented by rather dubious characters, had been going with Harry-the-Squint's sister for a year. . . ."

The magistrate still didn't understand. And Maigret said modestly, effacing himself as much as his massive frame would allow:

"Harry-the-Squint has been sentenced three times for burglary. He's an ex-bricklayer whose specialty is tunneling through walls. . . ."

And, with his hand on the door:

"Didn't the burglars on Rue Saint-Martin get in via the basement by tunneling through two walls? Good-by, sir . . ."

He was in a bad mood, all the same. That letter from Charlotte . . . And looking at him, you would have sworn that it wasn't only anger, but that he was also a little sad.

He could have sent an inspector. But would an inspector have been able to get the feel of the house as well as he could?

It was a large, new luxury building, the walls painted white, with a wrought-iron gateway, on Avenue du Madrid, near the Bois de Boulogne. The concierge's lodge, to the right of the entrance, had a glass door and was furnished like a reception room. Three women were dozing on chairs. A tray held a mound of visiting cards. Another woman, with red-rimmed eyes, opened the door and asked:

"What do you want?"

The door of a room farther down was open, and one could see a corpse laid out on the bed, hands folded, a rosary clasped in the fingers; two candles flickered in the dim light and a branch of boxwood had been dipped in a bowl of holy water.

Hushed voices, blowing of noses, tiptoing back and forth. Maigret made the sign of the cross, sprinkled some holy water over the body, and stood there for a minute, silently contemplating the dead man's nose, which the candles threw into strange relief.

"It's terrible, Superintendent. . . . Such a good man, not an enemy in the world!"

Above the bed, in an oval frame, there was a large photograph of Justin Colleboeuf, in his sergeant major's uniform, taken at a time when he still sported a large mustache. A *croix de guerre* with three palms and the military medal were fixed to the frame.

"He was in the regular army, Superintendent. When he reached retirement age, he didn't know what to do with himself, and he insisted on looking for a job. First he was night watchman at a club on Boulevard Haussmann. Then someone suggested the job of night concierge at the Majestic, and he took that. You see, he seemed to need very little sleep. At the barracks he used to get up nearly every night to make the rounds."

Her neighbors, or possibly relations, nodded sympathetically.

"What did he do during the daytime?" Maigret asked.

"He got home at a quarter past seven in the morning, just in time to put out the garbage cans for me; he wouldn't let me do any of the heavy work. Then he stood in the doorway and smoked a pipe while he waited for the postman, then had a little chat with him.

The postman had been in the same regiment as my husband, you see. After that he went to bed, till noon. That was all the sleep he needed. When he'd had his lunch, he walked across the Bois de Boulogne to the Champs-Elysées. Sometimes he went into the Majestic to say hello to his colleague on duty there during the day. Then he had his usual in the little bar on Rue Ponthieu, and got back at six o'clock, and left again at seven to go on duty at the hotel. He was so regular in his habits that people around here could set their clocks when they saw him go by. . . ."

"How long ago did he give up wearing a mustache?"

"He shaved it off when he left the army. I thought he looked very strange without it. . . . It made him seem less important. He even looked smaller, somehow."

Maigret bowed his head once more in the direction of the dead man and crept away on tiptoe.

He wasn't far from Saint-Cloud. He was impatient to get there, and yet, at the same time, for some unknown reason, he was stalling for time. A taxi went past. Oh, well! He held up his arm. . . .

"To Saint-Cloud . . . I'll explain where. . . ."

It was drizzling. The sky was gray. It was only three o'clock, but it might have been evening. The houses, in their bare little gardens with leafless winter trees, looked desolate.

He rang the bell. It was not Charlotte but Gigi who came to the door, while Donge's mistress peered from the kitchen to see who was there.

Still glowering balefully at him, Gigi let him in without saying a word. Only two days had passed since Maigret had last been there, and yet it seemed to him that the house looked different. Perhaps Gigi had brought some of her own chaos with her. The unwashed lunch dishes were still on the kitchen table.

Gigi was wearing one of Charlotte's dressing gowns, much too big for her, over her nightgown, and an old pair of shoes of Prosper's on her bare feet. She was smoking a cigarette and squinting through the smoke.

Charlotte, who had got up as he came in, was at a loss for words. She hadn't washed. Her skin looked blotchy, and, without a brassière, her bosom sagged.

He wondered who would speak first. They were exchanging anxious, suspicious looks. Maigret sat down, unabashed, with his bowler on his knee.

"I had a long talk with Prosper this morning," he said at last.

"What did he say?" Charlotte asked eagerly.

"That he didn't kill Mimi, or the night concierge."

"Ah!" Gigi cried triumphantly. "What did I tell you!"

Charlotte couldn't take it in. She seemed at a loss. She wasn't made for tragedy, and seemed perpetually to be looking for support.

"I also saw the magistrate. He has been sent an anonymous letter concerning Prosper and Mimi. . . ."

No reaction. Charlotte was still staring at him with curiosity, her lids heavy, her body limp.

"An anonymous letter?"

He handed her the recipe book, which he had brought with him.

"It's your writing in this book, isn't it?"

"Yes. Why?"

"Would you be good enough to take a pen? Preferably an old one that leaks. And paper and ink . . ."

There was a bottle of ink and a penholder on the dresser. Gigi looked from Maigret to her friend in turn, as if ready to intervene the moment she sensed danger.

"Make yourself comfortable . . . and write. . . ."

"What shall I write?"

93

"Don't write anything, Charlotte! You can't trust them. . . ."

"Write—there's no danger, I promise you—'*Sir, I am taking the liberty of writing to you about the Donge affair, which I read about in the newspaper . . . .*'

"Why do you spell newspaper with a *u*?"

"I don't know. . . . What should I have done?"

On the anonymous letter he had in his hand, there was no *u*.

" '*. . . The American woman isn't really an American woman; she was a dancer and her name was Mimi. . . .*' "

Maigret shrugged impatiently.

"That will do," he said. "Now, take a look. . . ."

The writing was exactly the same. Only the spelling mistakes were different.

"Who wrote that?"

"That's precisely what I would like to know. . . ."

"You thought it was me?"

She was choking with anger, and the Superintendent hurriedly tried to calm her.

"I didn't think anything. . . . What I came to ask you is, who, besides you and Gigi, knew about Prosper and Mimi's affair, and particularly about the child?"

"Can you think of anyone, Gigi?"

They took a long time thinking, in an idle fashion. They seemed to be drifting aimlessly in the untidy house, which had suddenly started to look seedy. Gigi's nostrils quivered from time to time, and Maigret realized that it wouldn't be long before she was out searching frantically for a fix.

"No . . . except us three . . ."

"Who was it who got Mimi's letter at the time?"

"It was me," said Gigi. "And before I left Cannes, I found it in a box where I kept some souvenirs. I brought it along."

"Let me see. . . ."

"Provided you promise . . ."

"Of course, you fool! Can't you see I'm trying to get Prosper out of this mess?"

He felt concerned, irritable. He began to have a vague sense that there were mysterious complications to the affair, but he did not have the slightest clue as to what they might be.

"Will you promise to give it back?"

He shrugged again, and read:

"My dear old Gigi,

"I've made it! I've made it at last! You and Charlotte laughed when I told you I'd get out of there and that I'd be a real lady.

"Well, I've done it. . . . Oswald and I were married yesterday, and it was a funny kind of wedding, because he wanted it to be in England, where it's quite different from what we do in France. In fact I sometimes wonder if I'm really married.

"Do tell Charlotte. We'll be sailing for America in three or four days, we don't know exactly when because of the strike.

"As for poor Prosper, I think it would be best not to tell him anything. He's a nice boy, but a bit simple. I don't know how I managed to stay with him for nearly a year. It must have been my girl-scout year.

"But still, he's done me a good turn, without knowing it. Keep this to yourself. No point in telling Charlotte–she's a great sentimental fool.

"I've known for some time that I was pregnant. You can imagine the face I made when I found out. I rushed to see a specialist before telling Oswald. We did some calculations. . . . Well, it's quite definite that the baby can't be Oswald's. So it's poor Prosper who . . . Don't ever let him know! He might get a rush of paternal feeling!

"It would take too long to tell you everything. The doctor has been very decent about it. By cheating a bit as to when the baby is

due (we'll have to pretend it's a premature delivery), we've succeeded in convincing Oswald that he's going to be a father.

"He took it very well. Contrary to what one might think when one first meets him, he's not such a fish. In fact, when we're alone together he acts like a child, and the other day, when we were in Paris, we went to all the amusement parks and rode on the merry-go-rounds.

"Well, I'm now Mrs. Oswald J. Clark of Detroit (Michigan), and from now on I'll have to speak English all the time, because Oswald, if you remember, doesn't know a word of French.

"I think of you two sometimes. Is Charlotte still worrying so much about getting fat? Does she still knit all the time? I bet she'll end up behind the counter in a needlework shop in the provinces!

"As for you, Gigi, old girl, I don't think you'll ever become respectable. As the creep in the white gaiters said so hilariously—you remember, the client who guzzled a whole bottle of champagne in one go?—you've got vice in the blood!

"Say hello to the Croisette for me, and don't burst out laughing when you look at Prosper and imagine he's a father without knowing it.

"I'll send you some postcards.

"Love and kisses,

"Mimi."

"May I take this letter with me?"

It was Charlotte who intervened.

"Let him, Gigi. . . . It can't make things any worse."

And as she showed the Superintendent out:

"Listen—couldn't I get permission to go and see him? He has the right to have his meals sent in from outside, doesn't he? Could you . . ."

She blushed and held out a thousand-franc note to him.

"If he could have a few books, too . . . He used to spend all his free time reading."

Rain. A taxi. The street lamps coming alight. The Bois de Boulogne, which Maigret had crossed on his bike, side by side with Donge.

"Drop me at the Majestic, please."

The concierge followed Maigret somewhat anxiously as he crossed the lobby without speaking, and took his coat and hat into the cloakroom. The manager had also seen him, through the gap in his curtains. Everyone knew Maigret, and they all followed him with their eyes.

The bar? Why not? He was thirsty. But he was attracted by the muffled sound of music. Somewhere in the basement a band was softly playing a tango. He went down a thickly carpeted staircase, into a bluish haze. Some people were eating pastry at little tables. Others were dancing. A waiter came up to the Superintendent.

"A beer, please . . ."

"We don't serve . . ."

Maigret gave him a look and hurriedly scribbled something on an order slip, then watched the route it took. At the back wall, to the right of the band, there was a sort of hatch in the wall.

On the other side were the glass cages, the pantry, the kitchens, the sculleries, the personnel dining room, and, right at the end, near the time clock, the cloakroom with its hundred metal lockers.

Someone was watching him—he could feel it—and he noticed Zebio dancing with a middle-aged woman who was dripping with jewels.

Was he imagining things? It seemed to Maigret that Zebio's look was intended to convey something to him. He turned and saw with a shock that Oswald J. Clark was dancing with his son's governess, Ellen Darroman.

They both seemed utterly oblivious of their surroundings. They were in the grip of new-found love. Solemn, hardly smiling, they were alone on the dance floor, alone in the world, and when the music stopped they stood transfixed for a minute before returning to their table.

Maigret then noticed that Clark was wearing a thin ribbon of black material on the lapel of his jacket—his way of showing mourning.

The Superintendent's fist tightened on Mimi's letter to Gigi, which was in his pocket. He had a terrible urge to . . .

But hadn't the magistrate told him not to get involved with Clark, who was, no doubt, too much of a gentleman to grapple with a policeman?

The tango was followed by a slow fox trot. A frothy beer followed the route the waiter's order had taken earlier, this time in the opposite direction. The pair were dancing again.

Maigret suddenly got up, forgot to pay for his beer, and hurried to the lobby.

"Is there anyone in Suite 203?" he asked the concierge.

"I think the nursemaid and the boy are up there. If you'd like to wait while I telephone . . ."

"No, please, don't do that. . . ."

"There's the elevator, just to your left, sir."

Too late. Maigret had made for a marble staircase and was slowly starting up the stairs, grunting as he went.

7

"What's He Saying?"

For a moment, Maigret was assailed by a strange thought, which, however, soon escaped him. He had reached the second floor of the Majestic and stopped for a moment to get his breath back. On his way up he had met a waiter with a tray, and a bellboy running up the stairs with a bundle of foreign newspapers under his arm.

On this floor there were smartly dressed women getting into the elevator, probably on their way to the tea dance. They left a trail of perfume behind them.

"They are all where they belong," he thought to himself. "Some behind the scenes and the others in the lobby and tearoom. The guests on one side and the staff on the other . . ."

But that wasn't what was bothering him, was it? Everyone all around him was in his allotted place, doing the right thing. It was normal, for instance, for a rich foreign woman to have tea, smoke cigarettes, and go out for fittings. It was natural for a waiter to carry a tray, a chambermaid to make beds, an elevator man to operate an elevator.

In short, their functions, such as they were, were clearly defined, settled once and for all.

But if anyone had asked Maigret what he was doing there, what would he have answered?

"I am trying to get a man sent to prison, or even executed."

It was nothing. A slight dizziness, probably caused by the overluxurious, almost aggressively luxurious setting, and the atmosphere in the tearoom.

Room 209 . . . 207 . . . 205 . . . 203 . . . Maigret hesitated for a moment and then knocked. His ear to the door, he could hear a child's voice saying a few words in English, then a woman's voice sounding more distant, and, he imagined, telling him to come in.

He crossed a little hall and found himself in a sitting room with three windows overlooking the Champs-Elysées. By one of the windows an elderly woman, in a white uniform like that of a nurse, was sitting and sewing. It was the nursemaid, Gertrud Borms, made to look even more severe by the glasses she wore.

But the Superintendent paid no attention to her. He was looking at a boy of about six, dressed in plus fours and a sweater that fitted snugly around him, including a large toy boat, and cars that were exact replicas of various real makes. There was a picture book on his knee, which he was looking at when Maigret came in, and after glancing briefly at the visitor, he bent over it again.

When he recounted the scene to Madame Maigret, the Superintendent's description went something like this:

"She said something like:

" 'You we you we we well . . .'

"And to gain time, I said very quickly:

" 'I hope that I'm correct in thinking this is Monsieur Oswald J. Clark's suite? . . .'

"She went on again:

" 'You we you we we well,' or something of the sort.

"And meanwhile I was able to get a good look at the boy. A very big head for his age, covered, as I had been told, with hair of a fiery red. The same blue eyes as Prosper Donge—the color of periwinkles or of certain summer skies. A thin neck . . .

"He started talking to his nursemaid, also in English, looking at me at the same time, and to me it still sounded like:

" 'You we you we we well . . .'

"They were evidently asking themselves what I wanted and why I was standing there in the middle of the room. I didn't know myself why I was there. There were flowers worth several hundred francs in a Chinese vase. . . .

"The nursemaid finally got up. She put her work down on the chair, picked up a telephone, and spoke to someone.

" 'Don't you understand any French, little fellow?' I asked the child.

"He merely stared at me with eyes full of suspicion. A few seconds later, an employee in a tail coat came into the suite. The maid spoke to him. He then turned to me.

" 'She wants to know what you want.'

" 'I wanted to see Monsieur Clark.'

" 'He isn't here. She says he is probably downstairs.'

" 'Thank you.' "

And that was that! Maigret had wanted to see Teddy Clark and he had seen him. He went back downstairs thinking about Prosper Donge, shut in his cell at the Santé. Automatically, without thinking, he went on down to the tearoom, and as his beer had not yet been cleared away, he sat down again. He was in a state of mind he knew well. It was sort of as if he were in a daze; he was conscious of what was happening around him, but without attaching any importance to it, without making any effort to place people or things in time or space.

Thus he saw a page go up to Ellen Darroman and say a few words to her. She got up and went to a telephone booth, in which she remained only for a few seconds.

When she came out, she immediately looked around for Maigret. Then she rejoined Clark and said something to him in a low voice, still looking at the Superintendent.

In that instant, Maigret had a sudden, very definite feeling that something disagreeable was about to happen. He knew that he had better leave at once, but he didn't go.

Had he been challenged to give his reasons, he would have found it hard to explain why he stayed there.

It wasn't because he felt it was his professional duty. There was no need to stay at the tea dance any longer—he was out of his element there.

That was precisely it—but he couldn't have put it into words. The magistrate had arrested Prosper Donge without consulting him, Maigret, hadn't he? And what was more, he had forbidden him to get mixed up with the American.

That was tantamount to saying:

"That is not your scene. . . . You don't understand it. . . . Leave it to me. . . ."

And Maigret, plebeian to the core, to the very marrow of his bones, felt hostile toward the world that surrounded him here.

Too bad. He would stay all the same. He saw that Clark was looking at him in turn, then frowned, and, no doubt telling his companion to stay where she was, got up. The music had struck up a new dance. The blue lighting gave way to pink. The American made his way between the couples and now stood in front of the Superintendent.

To Maigret, who couldn't understand a word of English, it still sounded like:

"Well you well we we well . . ."

But this time the tone was aggressive, and it was clear that Clark was having difficulty controlling himself.

"What are you saying?"

And Clark burst out even more angrily.

That evening, Madame Maigret said, shaking her head:

"Admit it! You did it on purpose! I know the way you have of looking at people! An angel would lose his temper."

He didn't admit anything, but there was a twinkle in his eye. Well, what *had* he done, anyway? He had stood there in front of the Yankee, with his hands in his jacket pockets, staring at him as if he found the spectacle curious.

Was it his fault? Donge was still uppermost in his mind—Donge, who was in prison, not dancing with the very pretty Miss Ellen. No doubt sensing drama in the air, she had got up to join them. But before she reached them, Clark had hit out furiously at Maigret's face, with the clean, clockwork precision one sees in American films.

Two women having tea at the next table got up screaming. Some of the couples stopped dancing.

Clark seemed to be satisfied. He probably thought that the matter was now settled once and for all.

Maigret didn't even deign to run his hand over his chin. The impact of Clark's fist on his jaw had been clearly audible, but the Superintendent's face remained as impassive as if he had been lightly tapped on the head.

Although he hadn't planned it that way, he was delighted at what had happened, and couldn't help smiling when he thought of the examining magistrate's face.

"Gentlemen! . . . Gentlemen! . . ."

Just as it seemed that Maigret would hurl himself at his adversary and that the fight would continue, a waiter intervened. Ellen and one of the men who had been dancing grabbed hold of Clark on either side and tried to restrain him, while he still went on shouting.

"What's he saying?" Maigret grumbled calmly.

"Never mind! Gentlemen, I beg you . . ."

Clark went on talking.

"What's he saying?"

Then, to everyone's surprise, Maigret began negligently to play with a shiny object that he had taken from his pocket, and the fashionable women stared in amazement at the handcuffs, which they had so often heard about but never actually seen.

"Waiter, please translate for me. Tell this gentleman that I am obliged to arrest him for assaulting an officer of the law on duty. And tell him, too, that if he is not prepared to follow me quietly, I shall, regretfully, have to use these handcuffs."

Clark didn't flinch. He didn't say another word, and pushed aside Ellen, who was clinging to his arm and trying to follow him. Without waiting for his hat and coat, he followed closely on the Superintendent's heels, and as they crossed the lobby, accompanied by a small crowd of the curious, the manager saw them from his office and raised his hands in horror.

"Taxi! . . . To the Palais de Justice . . ."

It was dark now. They went up the stairs, along corridors, and stopped outside Monsieur Bonneau's door. Maigret took on a humble and contrite attitude that Madame Maigret knew well and that always infuriated her.

"I am very sorry, sir. I have been obliged, much to my regret, to put Mr. Clark, whom you see here, under arrest."

The magistrate had no idea what had happened. He imagined that Maigret suspected the American of having murdered his wife and the night concierge.

"One moment, please! On what grounds have you . . ."

It was Clark who answered, and to Maigret the words still sounded like a senseless jingle.

"What's he saying?"

The poor magistrate raised his eyebrows and frowned. His own knowledge of English was far from good, and he himself had difficulty in following what the American was saying. He mumbled something, and sent his clerk to fetch another clerk who sometimes acted as interpreter.

"What's he saying?" Maigret muttered from time to time.

And Clark, irritated beyond measure by this, burst out, clenching his fists and imitating the Superintendent, "What's he saying? . . . What's he saying?," followed by another tirade in English.

The interpreter sidled into the room. He was a little bald man, disarmingly humble and timid. "He says he's an American citizen and that it's intolerable that policemen . . ."

Judging by his tone of voice, Clark had little respect for the police.

". . . that policemen should be allowed to follow him around everywhere. He says an inspector has been constantly at his heels."

"Is that true, Superintendent?"

"He is probably right, sir."

"He says another policeman was following Miss Ellen."

"It's very likely."

"And you burst into his hotel suite, in his absence."

"I knocked politely on the door and asked the good lady who was there in the most courteous way if I could see Monsieur Clark. After which I went down to the tea dance to have a glass of beer. It was then that this gentleman saw fit to shove his fist in my face."

Monsieur Bonneau was in despair. As if the affair wasn't complicated enough already! They had managed to keep the press out of it until now, but after the fracas in the tearoom, journalists would be besieging the Palais de Justice and Police Headquarters on all sides.

"I cannot understand, Superintendent, why a man like you, with twenty-five years' experience . . ."

And then he nearly lost his temper, because instead of listening to him, Maigret was playing with a bit of paper that he'd taken out of his pocket. It was a letter, written on bluish paper.

"Monsieur Clark certainly went too far. On the other hand, it is equally true to say that you failed to exercise the tact one would have expected of you in circumstances that . . ."

It had worked. Maigret had to turn away to hide his satisfaction. Clark had become hypnotized by the piece of paper, and finally walked up to him and held out his hand.

"Allow me . . ."

Maigret seemed startled and gave the American the piece of paper he was holding. The magistrate was more and more at a loss and suspected, not without reason, that the Superintendent was up to something.

Then Clark went up to the interpreter and showed him the letter, babbling away as he did so.

"What's he saying?"

"He says he recognizes his wife's handwriting and wants to know how you came to be in possession of a letter from her. . . ."

"Please explain, Monsieur Maigret," Monsieur Bonneau said coldly.

"I beg your pardon, sir. . . . It's a document that has just been given to me. . . . I wanted to show it to you, and add it to the dossier. Unfortunately Monsieur Clark took it before . . ."

Clark was still talking to the interpreter.

"What's he saying?" said the magistrate, catching the disease.

"He wants me to translate the letter. He says if someone has rifled through his wife's things, he will lodge a complaint with his embassy and that . . ."

"Translate it. . . ."

Maigret, his nerves taut, started filling his pipe, and went over to the window, where he could see the gas lamps shining like stars through their misty haloes.

The poor interpreter, his bald pate covered in sweat, translated Mimi's letter to her friend Gigi word by word, becoming so horrified as he went along that he wondered whether he dared to continue. The magistrate had drawn closer to read over his shoulder, but Clark, more peremptory than ever, had motioned him aside, saying:

"Allow me . . ."

He had the air of someone watching over his property, wanting to make sure the letter was not snatched away or destroyed, and that nothing was omitted in the translation. He pointed to each word with his finger, demanding the exact meaning.

Monsieur Bonneau, in complete despair, went over to join the Superintendent, who was smoking his pipe with seeming indifference.

"Did you do this on purpose, Superintendent?"

"How could I foresee that Monsieur Clark would thrust his fist in my face?"

"This letter explains everything!"

"With perfect cynicism!"

Good Lord! The magistrate had sent Prosper Donge to prison without any proof that he was guilty. And he was perfectly prepared to send Charlotte, Gigi, or any of the rest of them to join him!

The interpreter and Clark stood leaning over the table, where the green-shaded lamp shed its circle of light.

Finally Clark stood up. He banged his fist on the table, muttering something that sounded like:

"Damn!"

Then he reacted quite differently from what one might have expected. He remained calm, and didn't look at any of them. His face had set, and he stared into space. After a long period of this immobility, while the poor interpreter looked as though he was trying to gather his courage to apologize to him, he turned around, saw a chair in a corner of the room, and went and sat down, so calmly and simply that his very simplicity seemed almost tragic.

Maigret, who had been watching from a distance, could see beads of sweat literally breaking out on the skin above his upper lip.

Clark, at this moment, was somewhat like a boxer reeling from a knock-out blow but kept upright by the force of inertia, and instinctively looking for some support before going down for good.

There was complete silence in the magistrate's office, and they could hear the sound of a typewriter in a neighboring room.

Clark still made no move. He sat in his corner with his elbows on his knees, his chin in his hands, staring at his feet in their square-toed shoes.

After a long silence, they heard him mutter:

"Well! . . . Well! . . ."

And Maigret quietly asked the interpreter:

"What's he saying?"

The magistrate pretended to look at his papers. The smoke

from Maigret's pipe rose slowly in the air, seeming to drift toward the circle of light around the lamp.

"Well . . ."

Clark's thoughts were far away, God alone knew where. He finally looked up, and they wondered what he would do next. He took a heavy gold cigarette case out of his pocket, opened it, took out a cigarette, and snapped the case shut again. Then, turning to the interpreter, he said:

"Please . . ."

He wanted a match. The interpreter didn't smoke. The Superintendent handed him a box of matches, and as he took it, Clark glanced at him and gave him a long, eloquent look.

When he stood up, he must have felt weak, because his body seemed to sway a little. But he was still quite calm. His features were expressionless once more. He began by asking a question. The magistrate looked at Maigret as if waiting for him to answer.

"He asks if he may keep this letter?"

"I would rather it were photographed first. It won't take more than a few minutes. We can send it up to the Criminal Records Office. . . ."

Translation. Clark appeared to understand, nodded, and handed the letter to the clerk, who carried it away. Then he went on talking. It was maddening not to be able to understand. The shortest speech seemed to go on forever, and the Superintendent kept wanting to interrupt to ask what he was saying.

"First of all, he wants to consult his lawyer, because what he has just learned was totally unexpected and it changes everything."

Why did Maigret feel moved by these words? By this big healthy man who three days earlier had been riding on merry-go-rounds with Ellen, and only a few hours earlier had been dancing the tango in a haze of pink light, and now had received a blow much more shattering than the one he had dealt the Superintendent. And, like Maigret, he had barely flinched. He had sworn briefly, banged his fist on the table, then been silent for a while.

"Well . . . Well! . . ."

It was a pity they couldn't understand each other. Maigret would have liked to be able to talk to him.

"What's he saying now?"

"That he wants to offer a reward of a thousand dollars to the police officer who discovers the murderer."

While this was translated, Clark looked at Maigret as if to say:

"You see what a good sport I am. . . ."

"Tell him that the thousand dollars, if we win them, will go to the police orphanage."

It was odd. It was as though they were now competing to see who would be more considerate. Clark listened to the interpreter and nodded.

"Well . . ."

Then he began speaking again, this time in the tone of a businessman attending to his affairs.

"He supposes—but he doesn't want to do anything before having seen his lawyer—that an interview between him and this man—Prosper Donge—will be necessary. He asks if he might be permitted to do this and if . . ."

It was the magistrate's turn to nod gravely. And in another minute they would all have been exchanging compliments.

"Do go ahead. . . ."

"My fault entirely . . ."

"So sorry . . ."

Clark then asked a few additional questions, turning frequently to Maigret.

"He wants to know, sir, what is going to happen about his

hitting you, and if there will be any repercussions. He doesn't know what the law is in France in such a case. In his country . . ."

"Well, tell him I have no recollection of the incident he mentions. . . ."

The magistrate kept an anxious eye on the door. It was too good to be true! He was afraid some new incident might disrupt this marvelous harmony. If only they would hurry up and bring back the letter that . . .

They waited in silence. They had nothing more to say to each other. Clark lighted another cigarette, after having signaled to Maigret to lend him his matches.

At last the clerk came back with the fateful piece of blue paper.

"It's been copied, sir. May I?"

"Yes, give the letter to Monsieur Clark."

Clark slipped it carefully into his wallet, put the wallet into his breast pocket, and, forgetting he had come without his hat, looked around on the chairs. Then he remembered, smiled stiffly, and said good night to them all.

When the interpreter had also gone and the door was shut, Monsieur Bonneau cleared his throat two or three times, walked around his desk, and picked up some papers that he then didn't know what to do with.

"Was that what you wanted to happen, Superintendent?"

"What do you think, sir?"

"I believe it is I who am asking the questions."

"Of course, excuse me. You see, I have the feeling that it won't be long before Monsieur Clark remarries. . . . And the child is definitely Donge's son. . . ."

"The son of a man who is in prison and who is accused of . . ."

". . . Various crimes, yes," Maigret conceded. "But the boy

113

is nevertheless his son. What can I do under the circumstances? . . ."

He, too, looked for his hat, which he had left at the Majestic. He felt very odd leaving the Palais de Justice without it, so he took a taxi back to Boulevard Richard-Lenoir.

The bruise on his chin had had time to turn black. Madame Maigret spotted it at once.

"You've been fighting again!" she said, as she was setting the table. "And, of course, you're minus a hat! . . . What was it this time?"

He felt happy, and smiled broadly as he took his napkin out of its silver ring.

8

Maigret Dozing

And it wasn't at all bad, either, to be sitting comfortably at his desk, with the stove purring away at his back, and the window on the left curtained with lacelike morning mist, while in front of him was the black marble Louis-Philippe mantelpiece, with the clock whose hands had been permanently stuck at noon for the last twenty years; on the wall a photograph in a black-and-gilt frame of a group of gentlemen in frock coats and top hats, with improbable mustaches and pointed beards: the association of secretaries of the Central Police Station, when Maigret was twenty-four!

Four pipes were arranged in order of size on his desk.

A Rich American woman strangled in basement of Majestic.

The headline ran across the front page of the previous evening's paper. To journalists, of course, all American women are always rich. But Maigret's smile broadened on seeing a photograph of himself, in his overcoat and bowler hat, with his pipe in his mouth, looking down at something that wasn't shown in the picture.

Superintendent Maigret examines the corpse.

But it was a photograph that had been taken a year before, in the Bois de Boulogne, when he had in fact been looking at the body of a Russian who had been shot with a revolver.

Some more important documents, in Manila folders.

Report from Inspector Torrence as to inquiry regarding Monsieur Edgar Fagonet, alias Eusebio Fualdès, alias Zebio, aged twenty-four, born in Lille.

"Son of Fagonet, Albert Jean-Marie, foreman at the Lecoeur Works, deceased three years ago;

". . . and Jeanne Albertine Octavie Hautebois, wife of the above, aged fifty-four, housewife.

"The following information was given to us, either by the concierge at 57 Rue Caulaincourt, where Edgar Fagonet lives with his mother and sister, or by neighbors and shopkeepers in the area, or on the telephone by the police station in the Gasworks district of Lille.

"We have also been in touch by telephone with the Chevalet Sanatorium in Megève, and have personally seen the manager of the Imperia movie theater, on Boulevard des Capucines.

"Although opinion must be reserved until receipt of further verification, the information below appears to be correct.

"The Fagonet family, of Lille, were respectable people, living in a bungalow in the modern part of the Gasworks district. It appears that the parents' ambition was to give Edgar Fagonet a decent education, and, in fact, the latter went to the *lycée*, at the age of eleven.

"Shortly after, however, he had to take a year's leave and was sent to a sanatorium on the island of Oléron, on account of his health. His health apparently restored, he continued his studies, but from that time on they were constantly interrupted, owing to his weak constitution.

"When he was seventeen, it was found necessary to send him to a high altitude, and this time he spent four years at the Chevalet Sanatorium, near Megève.

"Doctor Chevalet remembers Fagonet well; he was a very good-looking boy and had a lot of success with some of the female patients. He had several affairs while he was there. It was also there that he became an accomplished dancer; the rules at the establishment were very relaxed, and it appears that in general the patients were bent on enjoying themselves.

"Rejected as unfit for service by the draft board.

"At twenty-one, Fagonet returned to Lille, just in time to close his father's eyes. The father left some small savings, but not enough to keep the family going.

"Fagonet's sister, Emilie, aged nineteen, has a bone disorder that has virtually disabled her. She is also mentally retarded, and needs constant care.

"It appears that on his return Edgar Fagonet made serious attempts to find regular employment, first in Lille and then in Roubaix. Unfortunately, his interrupted education was a handicap. On the other hand, although he was cured, his constitution made it impossible for him to engage in physical work.

"It was then that he came to Paris, where, a few weeks later, he could be seen, in a sky-blue uniform, working as usher at the Imperia movie theater, the first to employ young men instead of usherettes; they also hired a number of poor students.

"It is difficult to get precise information on this point, because those involved have proved discreet, but it appears certain that many of these young men, shown to advantage in their uniforms, made *PROFITABLE* conquests at the Imperia!"

Maigret grinned, because Torrence had found it necessary to underline the word *PROFITABLE* in red ink.

"At any rate, one of Fagonet's first actions—his friends were now beginning to call him Zebio, because of his Latin-American appearance—was to bring his mother and sister from Lille and install them in a three-room apartment, on Rue Caulaincourt.

"According to the concierge and the neighbors, he seems to be a particularly dutiful son, and it is often he who does the morning shopping.

"It was through colleagues at the Imperia that he learned, about a year ago, that the Majestic was looking for a professional dancing partner for its tearoom. He applied, and was taken on after a few days' trial. He then adopted the name Eusebio Fualdès, and the hotel management have no complaints to make about him.

"The staff say he is a rather timid, sentimental, and shy boy. Some of them call him 'the girl.' He doesn't talk much, and conserves his energy, since he's apt to have relapses; he is reported to have had to lie down on a bed in the basement for rest at various times, especially when he had to stay late on gala evenings.

"Although he gets along well with everyone, he doesn't seem to have any friends and is not much inclined toward gossip.

"It is thought that his monthly earnings, including tips, must be in the neighborhood of two thousand to two thousand five hundred francs.

"That just about sums up life in the household on Rue Caulaincourt.

"Edgar Fagonet doesn't drink, doesn't smoke, and doesn't take drugs. His poor health forbids it.

"His mother is from the north of France, a thickset, energetic woman. She has often spoken—to the concierge, for instance—about getting a job herself, but the care of her daughter has always prevented this.

"We have tried to find out if Fagonet has ever been at the Riviera, but were unable to establish precise information. It is said that he once went there for a few days, some three or four years ago, when he was still at the Imperia, accompanied by a middle-aged woman. But the information is too vague to be admitted as evidence."

Maigret slowly stuffed pipe number 3, filled up the stove, and went over to the window to have a look at the Seine, tinged with gold by a pale winter sun. Then, with a sigh of contentment, he sat down again.

Report by Inspector Lucas concerning Ramuel, Jean Oscar Adelbert, aged forty-eight, living in furnished rooms, 14 Rue Delambre (Fourteenth Arrondissement).

"Ramuel was born in Nice, of a French father, now deceased, and an Italian mother, whom we cannot trace, who seems to have returned to her native country some time ago. His father was a market gardener.

"At age eighteen, Jean Ramuel was working as a bookkeeper for a wholesaler in Les Halles, Paris, but we have been unable to check further into this, since his employer died ten years ago.

"He enlisted voluntarily at nineteen, left the army with the rank of quartermaster sergeant at twenty-four, and took a job with a broker, whom he left almost immediately to work as junior bookkeeper in a sugar refinery in Egypt.

"He stayed there three years, came back to France, took various jobs in the central area of Paris, and tried his luck on the Stock Exchange.

"At thirty-two, he embarked for Guayaquil, in Ecuador, hired by a Franco-English mining company to straighten out their accounts, which were in disorder.

"He was gone for six years. It was in Ecuador that he met Marie Deligeard, on whom we have scant information; most probably she was plying some disreputable trade in Central America.

"He brought her back with him. Since the company headquarters had by then been transferred to London, we have next to nothing on file for this period.

"The couple then lived for some time fairly comfortably in Toulon, Cassis, and Marseilles. Ramuel tried his hand at some real-estate deals, but without much success.

"Marie Deligeard, whom he introduced as Madame Ramuel, though they weren't married, is a loud-mouthed, vulgar woman, given to making scenes in public; she seems to take a malicious pleasure in making a spectacle of herself.

"They quarrel frequently, and Ramuel sometimes leaves his companion for several days, but it's always she who has the last word.

"Next, Ramuel and Marie Deligeard moved to Paris and rented a fairly comfortable furnished apartment on Rue Delambre: bedroom, kitchen, bathroom, and foyer, at eight hundred francs a month.

"Ramuel took a job as a bookkeeper in the Atoum Bank, on Rue Caumartin. (The bank has since crashed, but Atoum has started a carpet business on Rue des Saints-Pères, registered in the name of one of his employees.)

"Ramuel left the bank before the crash, and, in response to an advertisement, applied for the job of bookkeeper at the Majestic.

"He has been working there for the last three years. The management are perfectly satisfied with his work, but the staff don't like him, because he's excessively meticulous.

"Several times, after a quarrel with his companion, he has stayed at the hotel for a few days at a stretch without going home, sleeping on a makeshift bed. Nearly always there were telephone calls on these occasions, or else the woman came herself to take him home.

"The staff say they are astounded to see the abject terror she seems to inspire in him.

"Note that Jean Ramuel returned to the apartment on Rue Delambre yesterday."

A quarter of an hour later, the old page knocked softly on Maigret's door. Receiving no answer, he pushed the door quietly open and crept in on tiptoe.

The Superintendent seemed to be asleep. He was sprawled in his chair, with his vest unbuttoned and a cold pipe in his mouth.

The page was about to cough to announce his presence when Maigret mumbled without opening his eyes:

"What is it?"

"A gentleman to see you . . . Here's his card."

Maigret still seemed reluctant to shake off his drowsiness, and stretched out his hand with eyes still closed. Then, putting the visiting card down on his desk, he picked up the telephone.

"Shall I bring him in?"

"In a minute . . ."

He had barely glanced at the card: *Etienne Jolivet, assistant manager, Crédit Lyonnais, O Branch*.

"Hello! . . . Please ask Monsieur Bonneau, the examining magistrate, to let me have the name and address of Monsieur Clark's lawyer. . . . That's right. . . . When you've got it, call him for me, will you. . . . It's urgent."

For more than a quarter of an hour, the dapper Monsieur Jolivet, in striped trousers, black jacket, and hat as rigid as reinforced concrete, was poised very upright on the edge of his chair, in the gloomy waiting room at Police Headquarters. His companions were a sinister-looking youth and a streetwalker who was detailing her adventures in a raucous voice.

"Tell me, how could I have taken his wallet, without his noticing? . . . These provincials are all the same. They don't dare tell their wives how much they've spent in Paris, and so they pretend they've been robbed. It's lucky the Vice Squad superintendent knows me. That's telling enough, isn't it?"

"Hello! . . . Monsieur Herbert Davidson? . . . How do you do, Monsieur Herbert Davidson. Superintendent Maigret speaking . . . Correct . . . I had the pleasure of meeting your client Monsieur Clark yesterday. . . . He was most cooperative. . . . What's that? . . . No . . . not at all! . . . That's all forgotten. . . . I'm telephoning because I got the impression that he was prepared to help us to the best of his ability. . . . You say he's with you right now? . . .

"Could you ask him . . . I know that in his kind of world, and particularly in the United States, the partners in a marriage lead fairly separate lives. . . . Nevertheless, he may have noticed . . . No, just a minute . . . Wait, Monsieur Davidson, you can translate for him afterwards. . . . We know that Mrs. Clark received at least three letters from Paris during the last few years. I want to know if Monsieur Clark saw them. And I also particularly want to know if by any chance she received any further letters of the same kind. Yes . . . I'll hang on. . . . Thank you . . ."

He heard a murmur of voices at the other end of the line.

"Yes? . . . He didn't open them? . . . He didn't ask his wife what they were about? . . . Naturally! How very strange . . ."

He would like to see Madame Maigret getting letters without showing them to him!

"About one every three months? . . . Always in the same

handwriting? . . . A Paris postmark? . . . Just a minute, Monsieur Davidson . . ."

He went and opened the door of the inspectors' room because they were making a terrible racket.

"Shut up, will you!"

Then he came back.

"Yes . . . Fairly substantial sums? . . . Would you be good enough, Monsieur Davidson, to make a written statement of these details and send it to the examining magistrate? . . . No, that's all. . . . I apologize. . . . I don't know how the papers got hold of it, but I can assure you I had nothing to do with it. Only this morning I got rid of four journalists and two photographers who had been waiting to ambush me in the corridor at Police Headquarters. Please give my regards to Monsieur Clark. . . ."

He frowned. When he had opened the door of the inspectors' room just now, he had thought he recognized . . . He looked in again, and there, sitting on the table, were a reporter and his photographer colleague.

"Listen, young fellow. . . . I'm afraid I was shouting loud enough for you to hear me just now. . . . If a single word of what I said gets printed in your rag, that's the end of any information out of me. Understand?"

But he was half smiling as he went back to his room and rang for the page.

"Bring in Monsieur . . . Monsieur Jolivet. . . ."

"Good morning, Superintendent. Forgive me for bothering you. I thought I ought . . . When I read the paper yesterday evening . . ."

"Please sit down. . . ."

"I should add that I didn't come here on my own initiative, but after consultation with our head manager, whom I telephoned first thing this morning. . . . The name Prosper Donge struck

125

me, because I happened to have seen the name somewhere recently. I should explain that it's my job at the O Branch to countersign the checks. They go through automatically, of course, since the customer's account has been checked previously. I just glance at them, stamp them. . . . However, as a large sum of money was involved . . ."

"Just a minute . . . Do you mean Prosper Donge was a customer of yours?"

"He has been for the past five years, Superintendent. And even before that, because his account was transferred to us at the beginning of that period by our Cannes branch."

"May I ask you a few questions? . . . It will make it easier for me to straighten out my thoughts. Prosper Donge was a customer at your Cannes branch. . . . Can you tell me the size of his account at that time?"

"A very modest account, like those of most of the hotel employees who are our clients. However, one has to consider that as they get their board and lodging free, they can put aside the greater part of their earnings if they are thrifty. It was so in Donge's case, and he paid about a thousand to fifteen hundred francs into his account each month.

"Added to this, he had just got twenty thousand francs cash from a bond that had come to maturity. So he had about fifty-five thousand francs in his account when he came to Paris."

"And he continued to deposit small amounts?"

"Well—I've brought a list of his transactions with me. There's something rather upsetting about it, as you will see. In the first year, Donge, who was living in a small apartment on Rue Bray, near the Etoile, deposited another twelve thousand francs.

"The second year, he made withdrawals and no deposits at all. He changed his address. He went to live in Saint-Cloud, where, as I gathered from the checks he wrote, he was having a house built. Checks to the real-estate agent, to the carpenter, to the decorators, to the builders.

"So by the end of that year, as you can see from this statement, he only had eight hundred and thirty-three francs and a few centimes left in his account.

"Then, three years ago, that is a few months later . . ."

"Excuse me—you said *three years ago?*"

"That's right. . . . I'll give you the exact dates in a minute. Three years ago, he sent a letter notifying us that he had moved and asking us to take note of his new address: 117b Rue Réaumur."

"Just a minute . . . have you ever seen Donge in person?"

"I may have seen him, but I don't remember. . . . I'm not at the counter. I have a private office where I see the public only through a sort of spyhole."

"Have your employees seen him?"

"I asked several of the staff that question this morning. One of the clerks remembers him, because he was also having a house built in the suburbs. He told me he remembered remarking that Donge had left his house almost before it had been built."

"Could you get this man on the telephone?"

He did so. Maigret took the opportunity of stretching, like someone who is still half asleep, but his eyes were alert.

"You were saying . . . Let me see. . . . Donge changed his address and went to live at 117b Rue Réaumur. Would you excuse me a moment?"

He disappeared in the direction of the inspectors' office.

"Lucas . . . Jump in a taxi . . . 117b Rue Réaumur . . . Find out all you can about Monsieur Prosper Donge. . . . I'll explain later."

He came back to the assistant branch manager.

"What transactions did Donge make after that?"

"That's what I wanted to see you about. I was horrified, this morning, when I looked at his account, and even more horrified when I saw the last entry. The first American check . . ."

"Excuse me—the what?"

"Oh—there were several! The first American check, drawn on a bank in Detroit and made out to Prosper Donge, was dated March, three years ago, and made out for five hundred dollars. I can tell you what that was worth, exactly, at the time. . . ."

"It doesn't matter!"

"The check was paid into his account. Six months later another check for the same amount was deposited by Donge, and credited to his account."

The assistant manager was uncomfortably conscious that the Superintendent no longer appeared to be listening to him. And Maigret's thoughts were indeed far away. It had suddenly occurred to him, with some self-satisfaction, that if he hadn't telephoned the lawyer before seeing his visitor, if he hadn't asked certain questions when he was speaking to him, it would all have looked like sheer coincidence. . . .

"I'm listening, Monsieur—Monsieur Jolivet, isn't it?"

He had to look at the visiting card each time he said it.

"Or, rather, I already know what you are going to tell me. Donge continued to receive checks from Detroit, at the rate of about one every three months. . . ."

"That is correct. But . . ."

"The checks amounted to how much altogether?"

"Three hundred thousand francs . . ."

"Which remained in the bank without Donge's ever making any withdrawals?"

"That's right. But for the last eight months, there has been no check."

Ah! Hadn't Mrs. Clark been on a cruise in the Pacific, with her son, before coming to France?

"Did Donge continue to pay small amounts into his account during this time?"

"I can't find any trace of such deposits. Of course, any such sums would have been picayune compared to the American checks. But I'm just coming to the worrisome part. The letter the day before yesterday . . . It wasn't I who dealt with it; it was the head of the foreign-currency department—you'll see why in a minute. Well, we got this letter from Donge the day before yesterday. Instead of sending a check as usual, he asked us to make one out for him, payable to the bearer at a Brussels bank. It's a perfectly normal procedure. People going abroad often ask us for a check payable at another bank, which obviates problems with letters of credit and also makes it unnecessary to carry large sums in cash."

"What was the amount of this check?"

"Two hundred and eighty thousand French francs, almost the entire sum in his account. Actually, the balance left in Donge's account is now less than twenty thousand francs."

"You provided him with the check?"

"We sent it to the address he gave, as requested."

"Which was?"

"Monsieur Prosper Donge, 117b Rue Réaumur, as usual."

"So the letter would have been delivered this morning?"

"Probably . . . But in that case, Donge can't be in possession of it."

And the assistant manager brandished the newspaper.

"He can't have got it, because, the day before yesterday, at just about the time when we were mailing the check, Prosper Donge was arrested!"

Maigret leafed rapidly through the telephone directory and discovered that 117b Rue Réaumur, where several numbers were listed, also had a telephone in the concierge's lodge. He dialed the number. Lucas had arrived there a few minutes earlier.

He gave him brief instructions.

"A letter, yes, addressed to Donge . . . The envelope is stamped with the address of the O Branch of the Crédit Lyonnais. Make it snappy. Call me back."

"I think, Superintendent," said the assistant branch manager solemnly, "I did right to . . ."

"Of course, of course!"

But he was no longer aware of the poor fellow, and paid not the slightest attention to him. He was miles away, as if in a dream, and had to keep moving objects around, stirring up the stove, walking back and forth.

"A man from the Crédit Lyonnais, sir . . ."

"Tell him to come in. . . ."

As he spoke, the telephone rang. The bank clerk stood nervously in the doorway, staring in dismay at his assistant manager and wondering what he could possibly have done to be summoned to the Quai des Orfèvres.

"Lucas?"

"Well, Chief, the building isn't an apartment house. It's only offices, most of them with only one room. Some of them are rented by businessmen from the provinces, who find it useful to have a Paris address. Some of them practically never set foot in the place and have their mail forwarded from here. Others have a typist to answer the telephone.

"Three years ago, Donge had an office here for two months, at a monthly rent of six hundred francs. He came here only two or three times. Since then he has sent the concierge one hundred francs each month with instructions to forward his mail."

"What's the forwarding address?"

"*Poste restante* at the Jem Bureau, 42 Boulevard Haussmann."

"And the name?"

"The envelopes are self-addressed, and Donge sends them in advance. Wait—it's a bit dark in the lodge. Yes, put the light on, will you? Here we are. . . . J. M. D., *Poste restante*, Jem, 42 Boulevard Haussmann. That's all. Private bureaus are allowed to accept letters addressed with initials only."

"Did you keep your taxi? . . . No? . . . Idiot! Jump into a cab. What time is it? . . . Eleven . . . Get over to Boulevard Haussmann. Did the concierge forward a letter yesterday morning? . . . He did? Hurry, then. . . ."

He had forgotten the two men, who didn't know what to do and were listening in bewilderment. His thoughts had raced ahead so fast that he almost found himself asking:

"What are you two still doing here?"

Then he suddenly calmed down.

"What's your job at the bank?" he asked the clerk, who started in surprise.

"I'm in current accounts."

"Do you know Prosper Donge?"

"Yes, I know him. . . . That is, I've seen him several times. He was having a house built in the suburbs at one time, and so was I. Only I chose a site at . . ."

"Yes, yes. Go on. . . ."

"He used to drop in from time to time to draw small amounts in cash for the workmen who didn't have bank accounts and wouldn't accept checks. He found it very tiresome. I remember we discussed it. We said everyone should have a bank account, as they do in America. It was difficult for him to get to the bank, since he had to be at the Majestic from six in the morning until six at night, and the bank was shut by then. I told him—the assistant manager won't mind, because we do it for some of our clients—that he could just telephone me and I would send him the money to be signed for on receipt. I sent him money like that to the Majestic two or three times."

"Have you seen him since?"

"I don't think so. But I had to go to Etretat for two summers in a row, to run the branch there. He could have come in then."

Maigret pulled open one of his desk drawers, took out a photograph of Donge, and laid it on the desk silently.

"That's him! said the bank clerk. You couldn't miss his face. He told me that he had smallpox as a child and the farm people he was living with didn't even call in a doctor."

"Are you sure that's him?"

"Absolutely positive!"

"And you'd recognize his writing?"

"I would certainly recognize it," the assistant manager put in, annoyed at being relegated to second place.

Maigret handed them various bits of paper, with writing by different people on them.

"No! . . . No! . . . That's not his writing. . . . Ah! . . . Wait a minute. . . . There's one of his 7's. . . . He had a very characteristic way of writing his 7's. . . . And his *F*'s, too . . . That's one of his *F*'s!"

The writing they were pointing at was indeed Donge's; it was one of the slips he scrawled when people ordered so many coffees, coffees with croissants, teas, portions of toast, or cups of chocolate.

The telephone remained silent. It was just noon.

"Well, thank you very much, gentlemen!"

What on earth was Lucas doing at the Jem Bureau? It would be just like him to have gone by bus, to save the taxi fare!

9

Monsieur Charles's Newspaper

Singly, they might have passed without arousing attention. But standing together at the entrance to Police Headquarters, they looked as if they were waiting at a factory gate, a grotesque, pathetic pair. Gigi perched on her thin legs, in her worn rabbit-skin coat, her eyes wary, defying the policeman on duty at the entrance and peering to see who it was whenever she heard anyone coming; and poor Charlotte, too woebegone to do her hair properly or put on makeup, her large moonface blotched and red from crying; she was still sniffling into the bargain. Her nose was bright red, and sat like a small red ball in the middle of her face.

She was wearing a decent black cloth coat, with an astrakhan collar and a band of astrakhan around the hem. She held on limply to a large kid handbag. Without the ghoulish presence of Gigi, and the red nose gleaming in the middle of her face, she might have looked fairly presentable.

"There he is!"

Charlotte hadn't budged, but Gigi had been walking back and

forth in a frenzy. Now she saw Maigret coming, together with a colleague. He noticed the two women too late to make an escape. It was sunny out on the quay, with a touch of spring in the air.

"Excuse me, Superintendent. . . ."

He shook hands with his colleague.

"Have a good lunch, my dear fellow."

"Can we talk to you for a minute, Superintendent?"

And Charlotte burst into tears, pressing her handkerchief, which was rolled in a ball, to her mouth. People in the street turned around. Maigret waited patiently. Gigi, as if to excuse her friend, said:

"The magistrate sent for her, and she's just been seeing him. . . ."

Oh dear—Monsieur Bonneau! He had a right to summon her, of course. But all the same . . .

"Is it true, sir, that Prosper has . . . has admitted everything?"

This time Maigret smiled openly. Was that all the magistrate had been able to think up? That corny old trick used by junior policemen? And that big goose Charlotte had believed him!

"It's not true, is it? I knew it wasn't! If you knew what he said to me! . . . To listen to him you'd think I was the absolute dregs!"

The policeman on duty at the entrance was watching them with amusement. It was a curious sight—Maigret besieged by the two women, one of them crying, and the other glowering at him with no attempt to hide her antagonism.

"As if I'd write an anonymous letter accusing Prosper, when I'm sure he didn't kill her! . . . If it had been done with a gun, now, I might just have believed it. But not strangling someone . . . And doing it again the next day to some poor, innocent man who had done nothing! Have you come up with something new, Superintendent? Do you think they'll keep him in prison?"

Maigret waved to a taxi that was passing.

"Get in!" he told the two women. "I was going on an errand—you can come along."

It was quite true. At last Lucas had called, after having drawn a blank at the Jem Bureau. They were to meet at Boulevard Haussmann. And he had just had the idea that he might . . .

Both the women tried to sit on the jump seat, but he made them sit on the back seat, and he himself sat with his back to the driver. It was one of the first fine days of the year. The streets of Paris lay gleaming in the sun, and everyone looked cheerful.

"Tell me, Charlotte, is Donge still depositing his savings in the bank?"

He felt irritated by Gigi, who frowned each time he opened his mouth, as if suspecting a trap. She was clearly longing to say to her friend:

"Watch out! . . . Think before you answer!"

But Charlotte exclaimed:

"Savings! Poor darling! We haven't saved anything for a long time now! Since we've had that house on our necks, and that's a fact! . . . It was supposed to have cost forty thousand francs at the most, according to the estimates. First, the foundations cost three times more than they expected, because they found a subterranean stream. Then, when the walls were being built, there was a strike that brought everything to a stop just as the winter started. Five thousand francs here, three thousand francs there, they skinned us alive! If I told you how much the house has cost us so far, you wouldn't believe it! I don't know the exact figure, but it must be well above eighty thousand, and there are still some things that haven't been paid for."

"So Donge doesn't have any money in the bank?"

"He doesn't even have an account. He hasn't had one for

137

. . . wait a minute . . . for about three years now. I remember, because one day the postman brought a money order for about eight hundred francs. I didn't know what it was. When Donge got back he told me he had written to the bank to close his account."

"You can't remember the date?"

"What's that got to do with you?" asked Gigi, unable to refrain from injecting her sour note.

"I know it was in the winter, because I was busy breaking the ice around the pump when the postman came. Wait . . . I went to the Saint-Cloud market that day. I bought a goose. So it must have been a few days before Christmas."

"Where are we going?" grumbled Gigi, looking out of the window.

Just at that moment, the taxi stopped on Boulevard Haussmann, right at the corner of Faubourg Saint-Honoré. Lucas, standing on the sidewalk, was visibly surprised to see Maigret follow the two women out of the cab.

"One moment," the Superintendent told them.

He drew Lucas aside.

"Well?"

"You see that narrow shop, between the luggage store and the beauty shop? That's the Jem Bureau. It's run by a nasty old man who wouldn't give me any information. He wanted to shut the bureau and go out to lunch, pretending it was his lunch hour. I ordered him to stay. He's furious. He insists that I've got no right without a warrant. . . ."

Maigret went into the shop, so poorly lighted that it was almost dark, with a dirty wooden counter running down the middle. Small wooden pigeonholes, equally filthy, lined the walls, and these were full of letters.

"I'd like to know . . ." the old man began.

"I'll ask the questions, if you don't mind," Maigret growled. "You get letters addressed with initials only, I believe, which is not permitted in regular post offices, so your clientele must be a really nice bunch."

"I pay for my license," the old man promptly objected.

He wore glasses with heavy lenses, behind which darted rheumy eyes. His jacket was dirty, the collar of his shirt frayed and greasy. A rancid smell emanated from his body and permeated the whole shop.

"I want to know if you have a register, where you note the real names of your clients against the initials."

The man snickered.

"D'you think they'd come here if they had to give their names? Why not ask them for identity papers?"

It was somewhat unpleasant to think of pretty women coming furtively into the shop, which must have served as a go-between for a great many adulterous couples, as well as for other shady transactions.

"You received a letter yesterday morning addressed with the initials J. M. D."

"It's possible. I've already said so to your colleague. He even insisted on checking that the letter was no longer here."

"Then someone must have come to collect it. Can you tell me when?"

"I've got no idea, and even if I had, I doubt if I'd tell you."

"You realize I may come and close down your shop one of these days?"

"Other people have said the same to me, and my shop, as you call it, has been here for the last forty-two years. . . . If I counted up all the husbands who've come to shout at me, and who've even threatened me with their sticks . . ."

Lucas had been quite right in saying he was nasty.

"If it's all the same to you, I'll put up the shutters and go and have my lunch."

Where could the old brute possibly have lunch? Surely he didn't have a family—wife and children? It seemed far more likely that he was a bachelor, with his customary place at some dingy restaurant in the neighborhood, where his napkin was kept in a ring.

"Have you ever seen this man?"

Maigret, refusing to be hustled, produced Donge's photograph again, and curiosity gained the upper hand over the man's ill temper. He bent to peer at it and had to hold it within a few inches of his face. His expression didn't change. He shrugged.

"I don't remember seeing him . . ." he mumbled, as though disappointed.

The two women were waiting outside, in front of the narrow shopwindow. Maigret called Charlotte in.

"And do you recognize her?"

If Charlotte was acting, she was doing it remarkably well; she was looking around as if shocked and embarrassed, which was hardly surprising in such surroundings.

"What does it . . ." she began.

She was terrified. Why had she been brought here? She looked around instinctively for Gigi, who came in of her own accord.

"How many more people do you plan to bring in here?"

"You don't recognize either of them? You can't tell me whether it was a man or a woman who came to collect the letter addressed to J. M. D., or when the letter was collected?"

Without bothering to reply, the man seized a wooden shutter and started to put it up in front of the door. There was no option but to beat a hasty retreat. Maigret, Lucas, and the two women found themselves outside on the sidewalk, under the chestnut trees with their new spring buds.

"You two can go now!"

He watched them leave. Gigi had gone barely ten yards when she started violently haranguing her companion, whom she was dragging along at a pace little suited to Charlotte's dumpy figure.

"Any news, Chief?"

What could Maigret say? He was brooding, anxious. The spring weather seemed to make him irritable, rather than relaxed.

"I don't know. . . . Go and get yourself some lunch. Stay in the office this afternoon. Tell the banks—in France and Brussels— that if a check for two hundred and eighty thousand francs has been presented . . ."

He was only a few steps from the Majestic. He walked along Rue de Ponthieu, and into the bar near the service entrance of the hotel. They served snacks there, and he ordered some canned *cassoulet*, which he ate morosely, alone at a little table in the back, near two men who were discussing horses while hurriedly downing a snack before going to the races.

Anyone following him that afternoon would have had a hard time deciding exactly what Maigret was doing. Having finished his meal, he had some coffee, bought some tobacco, and filled his pouch. Then he walked out of the bar and stood on the sidewalk for a while, looking around.

He probably hadn't formulated any precise plan of action. Slowly he ambled into the Majestic and along the back corridor, stood by the time clock, rather like a traveler with hours to wait at a station, who puts coins into the candy machines.

People brushed past him, mostly cooks, with napkins around their necks, dashing out to have a quick drink at the bar next door.

As he advanced along the corridor, the heat grew more intense, and there was a strong smell of cooking.

The cloakroom was empty. He washed his hands at a basin, for no reason, to pass the time, and spent a good ten minutes cleaning his nails. Then, as he was too hot, he took off his overcoat and hung it in locker 89.

Jean Ramuel was sitting in state in his glass cage. In the breakfast kitchen opposite, the three women were working at an accelerated pace, with a new cook in a white jacket who had replaced Prosper.

"Who's that?" Maigret asked Ramuel.

"A 'temp' they've engaged until they find someone . . . He's called Monsieur Charles. So you've come to take a little stroll around, Superintendent? . . . Excuse me a minute. . . ."

It was hectic. The luxury clientele ate late, and the slips were piling up in front of Ramuel, waiters were dashing past, all the telephones were ringing at once, and the dumbwaiters were shooting up and down nonstop.

Maigret, still wearing his bowler, wandered around with his hands in his pockets, stopping by a cook who was thickening a sauce as if it fascinated him, watching the women wash up, or peering through the glass partitions into the personnel dining room.

He went up the back stairs, as he had done on his first visit, but this time he stopped on all the floors, in a leisurely fashion, still looking rather disgruntled. As he came down again, he was joined by the manager, who was out of breath.

"They've just told me you were here, Superintendent. I don't suppose you've had lunch? May I offer . . ."

"I've eaten, thank you."

"May I ask if you have any news? I was completely staggered

when they arrested Prosper Donge. But are you sure you won't have anything? A brandy, perhaps?''

The manager was growing more and more uncomfortable there in the narrow staircase with Maigret, who obstinately refused to show any reaction. There were times when the Superintendent gave the impression of being as thick-skinned and sleepy-looking as a pachyderm.

"I had hoped the press wouldn't get hold of the affair. You know how, for a hotel . . . As for Donge . . ."

It was hopeless. Maigret offered him no help as he stumbled on. He had started going downstairs again, and they had now reached the basement.

"A man whom, only a few days ago, I would have cited as of exemplary character. Because, as you may imagine, we get all sorts in a hotel like this. . . ."

Maigret was glancing from one glass partition to another, or, as he would have put it, from one aquarium to another. They finally ended up in the cloakroom, by the famous locker 89, where two human lives had come to an abrupt end.

"As for that poor Colleboeuf . . . Forgive me if I'm boring you. . . . I've just thought of something. . . . Don't you think it would require unusual strength to strangle a man in broad daylight, only a few steps from a lot of people—I mean so that the victim had no chance to cry out or struggle? It would be possible now, because everyone's rushing around making a lot of noise. But at half past four or five in the afternoon . . ."

"You were in the middle of your lunch, I imagine?" Maigret murmured.

"It doesn't matter. . . . We're used to eating whenever we can. . . ."

"Do please go and finish your meal. I'm leaving. . . . I'll just have a look. . . . If you'll excuse me . . ."

And he ambled off down the corridor again, opening and shutting doors and lighting his pipe, which he then allowed to go out.

His steps kept bringing him back to the breakfast kitchen; he came to know the occupants' every movement, and muttered between his teeth:

"So . . . Donge is there . . . he's there from six o'clock on every day. . . . OK, he has had a cup of coffee at home, which Charlotte prepares when she gets in. . . . OK . . . when he gets here, I imagine he pours himself a cup as soon as the first percolator heats up. . . ."

What did it all add up to?

"He usually takes a cup of coffee up to the night concierge. Yes . . . Actually, that day, Justin Colleboeuf probably came down, because it was ten past six and Donge still hadn't come up. So . . . well . . . for that or some other reason . . ."

They weren't filling the silver coffeepots that had been used at breakfast, but little brown glazed pots, each topped with a filter.

"Breakfasts go up all morning, more and more as it gets later. . . . Then Donge has a bite to eat himself. . . . It's brought to him on a tray. . . ."

"Would you mind moving a little to the right or left, Superintendent? You're blocking my view of the trays."

It was Ramuel, who had to oversee everything from his glass cage. Did he have to count all the cups leaving the breakfast kitchen as well?

"I'm sorry to have to disturb you. . . ."

"It's quite all right."

Three o'clock. The pace slackened a bit. One of the cooks had just got his coat to go out.

"If anyone asks for me, Ramuel, I'll be back at five. I've got to go to the tax bureau."

Nearly all the little brown coffeepots had come down again. Monsieur Charles came out of the breakfast kitchen and walked along the corridor leading to the street, not without glancing curiously at the Superintendent. The women must have told him who he was.

A few minutes later he returned with an evening paper. It was shortly after three. The women were washing dishes at the sink, up to their elbows in hot water.

Monsieur Charles, however, sat down at his little table, making himself as comfortable as possible. He opened the paper, put on his glasses, lighted a cigarette, and began to read.

There was nothing odd about this, but Maigret was staring at him as though thunderstruck.

Smiling, he said to Ramuel, who was counting his slips, "It looks as if there's a break now, is there?"

"Until half past four, then it starts up again with the tea dance. . . ."

Maigret stayed standing in the corridor for another moment. Then suddenly a bell rang in the breakfast kitchen, Monsieur Charles got up, spoke a few words into the telephone, reluctantly left his paper, and went off along the corridor.

"Where's he heading?"

"What time is it? Half past three? It's probably the storekeeper calling to give him his coffee and tea supplies."

"Does he do that every day?"

"Yes, every day . . ."

Ramuel watched Maigret, who was now calmly wandering into the breakfast kitchen. He did nothing spectacular—merely opened the drawer of the table, an ordinary deal one. He found a small bottle of ink, a penholder, and a package of writing paper.

There were also some pencil stubs and two or three postal order forms.

He was shutting the drawer when Monsieur Charles came back with some packages. Seeing Maigret bending over the table, he misinterpreted his action.

"You can take it," he said, meaning the newspaper. "There's nothing in it! I only read the serial and the employment ads."

Maigret had guessed as much.

"That's how it was. Prosper Donge sitting peacefully at his table . . . the three women over there splashing around at the sink . . . he . . ."

The Superintendent was now rapidly losing his ponderous and sleepy look. Like a man who suddenly remembers that he has an urgent job to do and doesn't bother about saying good-by, he walked rapidly toward the cloakroom, grabbed his coat, put it on as he came out, and a minute later had thrown himself into a taxi.

"Public Prosecutor's Department, Financial Section," he directed the driver.

A quarter to four. Someone might still be on duty. If all went well, there was a chance that by tonight . . . before the day was over . . .

He turned around. The taxi had just driven past Edgar Fagonet, alias Zebio, on his way to the Majestic.

10

Dinner at the Coupole

The operation was carried out with such brutal efficiency that even an ancient antique dealer, rotting away at the back of his dark little shop like a mole, came to the door, dragging his feet over the floorboards.

It was a few minutes to six. The dingy shops on Rue des Saints-Pères were feebly lighted, and outside in the street there lingered a bluish twilight.

The police car shot around the corner with enough blasts on the horn to unnerve all the antique dealers and small shopkeepers in the street.

Then, with a squeal of brakes, it drew up to the curb, and three men jumped out, looking purposeful, as if summoned by an emergency call.

Maigret walked up to the door, alone, just as the pale, terrified face of a shop assistant glued itself to the glass, like a decal. An inspector went up the side alleyway to check that the shop had no other entrance; the policeman stationed on the sidewalk, with his large, drooping mustache and baleful, suspicious eyes, looked more like a caricature than a real inspector, for which reason he had been purposely chosen by Maigret.

In the shop, its walls hung with Persian carpets that gave it an air of opulent tranquillity, the assistant tried to appear calm.

"Did you want to see Monsieur Atoum? . . . I'll see if he's in. . . ."

But the Superintendent had already brushed the poor creature aside. He had spotted a glow of reddish light issuing from a gap between the carpets at the back of the shop, and could hear the murmur of voices. He found himself on the threshold of a small room, no bigger than a tent, made of four carpets and furnished with a sofa covered with bright leather cushions, and a table inlaid with mother-of-pearl, on which cups of Turkish coffee were set out.

A man who had got up and was about to leave seemed as ill at ease as the clerk. Another man, reclining on the sofa, was smoking a gold-tipped cigarette and said a few words in a foreign tongue.

"Monsieur Atoum, I believe? Superintendent Maigret of the Police Judiciaire."

The visitor hurriedly departed, and there was a slam as the door of the shop closed behind him. Maigret seated himself composedly on the edge of the sofa, examining the little Turkish coffee cups with interest.

"Don't you recognize me, Monsieur Atoum? We spent all of a half day together, let me see . . . good Lord, it must be nearly eight years ago now. . . . A splendid journey! The Vosges, Alsace! If I remember rightly, we parted company near a frontier post."

Atoum was fat, but his face was still young, and he had magnificent eyes. He was richly dressed, with rings on his

150

fingers, and heavily scented, and he reclined, rather than sat, on the divan. The small room, lighted by a mock-alabaster lamp, was more like something out of an Oriental bazaar than a Paris street.

"Let me see—what was it you had been up to at the time? Nothing very serious, as far as I remember. But as your papers weren't in order, the French government thought it would be well advised to offer you a little trip to the border. You came back that very evening, of course, but appearances were saved, and I think you then found protection."

Atoum seemed quite unperturbed by all this, and kept staring at Maigret with feline calm.

"Later you went into banking, because in France you don't necessarily have to have a clean slate to handle people's money. You've had various little difficulties since, Monsieur Atoum."

"May I be allowed to ask, Superintendent . . ."

"What I'm doing here, you mean? Well, frankly, I don't know. I've got a car and some men outside. We may all go for a little ride."

Atoum's hand remained perfectly steady as he lighted a cigarette, having offered one to Maigret, who refused.

"Or I could leave without fuss, and let you stay here."

"Depending on what?"

"The way you answer one small question . . . I know how discreet you are, so I've taken a few precautions to help you overcome this, as it were. When you were in banking, you had a clerk as your right-hand man, your trusted confidant—you note I don't say accomplice—by the name of Jean Ramuel. Well—I'd like to know why you parted with such a trusted helper, why, to be more precise, you kicked him out?"

There was a long silence while Atoum reflected.

"You're mistaken, Superintendent. I didn't get rid of Ramuel;

151

he left of his own accord, for reasons of health, I think it was."

Maigret got up.

"Too bad! In that case it'll have to be the first alternative. If you'd be good enough to come with me, Monsieur Atoum . . ."

"Where are you going to take me?"

"Back to the border . . ."

A trace of a smile showed on Atoum's face.

"But we'll try a different border this time. I think I'd like to make a little trip to Italy. I'm told that you left that country somewhat in haste, forgetting to serve a five-year sentence for forgery and passing counterfeit checks. So . . ."

"Sit down, Superintendent. . . ."

"You think it won't be necessary for me to get up again in a hurry, then?"

"What do you want with Ramuel?"

"Perhaps to see that he gets what is coming to him. What do you think?"

And changing his tone abruptly:

"Come, Atoum! I've got no time to waste today. I have no doubt Ramuel's got a hold over you. . . ."

"I admit that if he were to talk inadvisedly, he could cause me a great deal of trouble. Banking affairs are complex. He had a habit of sticking his nose into everything. . . . I wonder if I wouldn't do better to choose Italy. . . . Unless you can give me some assurance . . . that if, for example, he mentions certain affairs, you won't pay any attention to them, since that's all in the past and I'm now an honest businessman . . ."

"It's within the realm of possibility."

"In that case I can tell you that Ramuel and I parted company after a somewhat stormy exchange of words. I had discovered, in

152

fact, that he was working in my bank for his own purposes, and that he had committed a number of forgeries. . . ."

"I suppose you kept the documents?"

Atoum batted his eyelids, and confessed in a whisper:

"But he has kept others, you see, so . . ."

"So you've got a mutual hold over each other. Well, Atoum, I want you to give me those documents immediately. . . ."

Atoum still hesitated. Italian or French prison? He finally got up and lifted the hanging behind the sofa, revealing a little safe set in the wall, which he opened.

"Here are some bills of exchange on which Ramuel copied not only my signature, but also that of two of my clients. If you find a little red book among his things, in which I noted various transactions, I would appreciate it if . . ."

And as he crossed the shop after Maigret, he hesitated a moment and then, pointing to a magnificent Karamani carpet:

"I wonder if Madame Maigret would like that design. . . ."

It was half past eight when Maigret walked into the Coupole and made for the part of the vast room where dinner was being served. He was alone, his hands in his pockets, as usual, and his bowler on the back of his head. He seemed to have nothing on his mind except looking for a free table.

Then he suddenly saw a small man, already installed with a grilled chop and a glass of beer in front of him.

"Hello, Lucas! May I share your table?"

He sat down, smiling in anticipation of his dinner, and then got up again to hand his coat to a waiter. An aggressive and vulgar-looking woman, at the table next to him, with a half lobster of impressive dimensions on her plate, shouted in a grating voice:

"Waiter! Some fresh mayonnaise! This smells of soap!"

Maigret turned toward her, and then to the man at her side, and said with a show of genuine astonishment:

"Why . . . Monsieur Ramuel! What a coincidence meeting you here! Would you do me the honor of introducing . . . ?"

"My wife . . . Superintendent Maigret, of the Police Judiciaire."

"Delighted to meet you, Superintendent."

"Steak and chips, and a large beer, please, waiter!"

He glanced at Ramuel's plate and saw that he was eating noodles, without butter or cheese.

"Do you know what I'm thinking?" he said suddenly, in a friendly tone of voice.

"It seems to me, Monsieur Ramuel, that you've always been unlucky. It struck me the first time I saw you. There are some people for whom nothing goes right, and I've noticed that on top of all that, those very same people are victims of the most unpleasant illnesses and accidents."

"He'll take what you say as an excuse for his horrible disposition!" interrupted Marie Deligeard, sniffing the new mayonnaise she had just been brought.

"You're intelligent, well educated, and hard working," continued the Superintendent, "and you should have made your fortune ten times over. And the strange thing is that you came very close, more than once, to securing a splendid position for yourself. In Cairo, for instance . . . Then in Ecuador . . . Each time, you were a rapid success, and then had to go right back where you started again. What happens when you get an excellent job in a bank? You have the bad luck to fall in with a crooked banker—Atoum—and are obliged to leave."

The people dining at the neighboring tables had no idea what they were talking about. Maigret spoke in a cheerful, friendly tone of voice and attacked his steak with relish, while Lucas kept his nose buried in his plate, and Ramuel appeared to be busy with his noodles.

"In fact, I wasn't expecting to meet you here, on Boulevard Montparnasse; I thought you'd already be on the train to Brussels."

Ramuel said nothing, but his face turned even more yellow, and his fingers tightened on his fork. His companion shouted at him:

"What? You were going to Brussels without telling me? What's up, Jean? Another woman, eh?"

And Maigret said blandly:

"I assure you, madame, that it's got nothing to do with a woman. Don't worry. But your husband . . . I mean your friend . . ."

"You can call him my husband. I don't know what he's told you on that score, but we're really and truly married. I can prove . . ."

She fumbled frantically in her bag and pulled out a tightly folded, torn, and faded scrap of paper.

"There you are! It's our marriage certificate!"

The text was in Spanish, and it was covered with Ecuadorian stamps and seals.

"Answer me, Jean! What were you going to Brussels for?"

"But . . . I had no intention . . ."

"Come now, Monsieur Ramuel. . . . Forgive me—I had no intention of causing a family row. When I learned that you had taken nearly all your money out of the bank and had asked for a check for two hundred and eighty thousand francs, to be drawn on Brussels . . ."

Maigret hurriedly bit into a mouthful of deliciously crisp

chips, because he was having difficulty not smiling. A foot had been placed on his, and he realized it was Ramuel's—silently begging him to be quiet.

It was too late. Forgetting her lobster, forgetting the dozens of people dining around them, Marie Deligeard—or, rather, Madame Ramuel, if the scrap of paper could be believed—shrieked:

"Did you say two hundred and eighty thousand francs? . . . Do you mean he had two hundred and eighty thousand francs in the bank and kept me short?"

Maigret looked pointedly at the lobster and half bottle of twenty-five-franc Riesling.

"Answer me, Jean! Is it true?"

"I have no idea what the Superintendent's talking about."

"You've got a bank account?"

"I repeat, I haven't got a bank account, and if I did have two hundred and eighty thousand francs . . ."

"What do you mean by saying that, then, Superintendent?"

"I'm sorry, madame, to upset you like this. I thought you knew about it, that your husband hid nothing from you. . . ."

"Now I understand!"

"His behavior recently . . . He was too kind. . . . Fawning on me . . . But I thought it didn't seem natural. . . . It was all part of the plan, was it!"

People were turning to stare at them in amusement, because all this could be heard at least three tables away.

"Marie! . . ." Ramuel begged.

"You were making your pile in secret, were you, and letting me go without, while you got ready to leave. . . . One fine day you'd have left, just like that! I'd find myself all alone in an apartment with the rent not even paid! None of that, my friend! You've tried to sneak away twice already, but as you know perfectly well, it didn't work. You're sure there's no woman tucked away somewhere, Superintendent?"

"Look, Superintendent, don't you think it would be better if we continued this conversation somewhere else?"

"Oh, no, not at all!" Maigret said. "Besides, I'd like . . . Waiter!"

He pointed to the silver dish with a domed cover that was being wheeled on a trolley between the tables.

"What have you got in that contraption?"

"Roast beef."

"Good! Cut me a slice, will you? A little beef, Lucas? . . . And some chips, please, waiter!"

"Take away my lobster—it's not fresh!" Ramuel's companion interrupted.

"Give me the same as the Superintendent. . . . So that bastard had money tucked away all the time, and . . ."

She had become so heated she had to touch up her face, waving a dubious-looking pink powderpuff over the tablecloth.

And under the table, there was frantic activity—Ramuel quietly kicking her to make her shut up, and she pretending not to understand and stabbing him viciously with her heel in return.

"You'll pay for this, you bastard! Just wait! . . ."

"Look, I'll explain it all, in a minute. . . . I don't know why the Superintendent thinks . . ."

"You—you're sure you're not mistaken? I know what you police are like. When you're stumped, you invent something just to make people talk. I hope that's not what you're up to?"

Maigret looked at his watch. It was half past nine. He gave Lucas a quiet wink, and Lucas coughed. Then Maigret leaned confidentially toward Ramuel and the woman.

"Don't move, Ramuel. Don't make a scene; it won't help. Your right-hand neighbor is one of our men. And Police Sergeant

157

Lucas has been following you since this afternoon, and it was he who let me know you were here. . . ."

"What do you mean?" stuttered Marie Deligeard.

"I mean, madame, that I wanted to let you finish your dinner first. I'm afraid I have to put your husband under arrest. And it will be better for everyone if we do it quietly. Finish your meal. We'll go out together in a minute—all good friends. We'll get a taxi and go for a little ride to the Quai des Orfèvres. You can't imagine how peaceful the offices are at night. Mustard, please, waiter! And some gherkins, if you have them!"

Marie Deligeard dug into her food with venom, giving her husband a withering look from time to time, her face contorted in a deep scowl, which didn't improve her looks or make her more attractive. Maigret ordered a third glass of beer and leaned across to Ramuel, murmuring confidentially:

"You see, at about four o'clock this afternoon, I suddenly remembered that you had been a quartermaster sergeant. . . ."

"You always said you were a second lieutenant!" the odious woman spat, not missing an opening.

"But it takes brains, madame, to be a quartermaster sergeant! It's the quartermaster sergeant who does all the writing for the company. So, you see, I thought back on my military service, which was a long time ago, as you can imagine. . . ."

Nothing could keep him from enjoying his chips. They were sensational—crisp outside and melting within.

"As our captain came to the barracks as little as possible, it was our quartermaster sergeant who signed all the passes and most other documents, in the captain's name, of course. And the signature was so well done that the captain could never tell which signatures he had written himself and which were the work of the quartermaster sergeant. . . . Do you see what I'm getting at, Ramuel?"

"I don't understand. . . . And as I can't imagine that you're going to try to arrest me without a proper warrant, I'd like to know . . ."

"I've got a warrant from the Financial Section of the Public Prosecutor's Department. Does that surprise you? It happens quite often, you know. You work on a case and quite by accident you uncover something else, something that happened some years ago and that everyone has forgotten. I've got some papers in my pocket, given to me by a man called Atoum. You are sure you don't want anything more to eat? No dessert, madame? . . . Waiter! We'll go Dutch, if you don't mind. How much is my share, waiter? I had a steak, something from the trolley, three portions of chips, and three beers. Do you have a light, Lucas?"

11

Gala Evening at Police Headquarters

The dark entry, then the great staircase, with dim lights at infrequent intervals, and finally the long corridor with its many doors.

Maigret said cheerfully to Marie Deligeard, who was out of breath:

"Here we are, madame. You can get your breath back."

There was only one light on in the corridor, along which two men were walking, deep in conversation—Oswald J. Clark and his lawyer.

At the end of the corridor was the waiting room, glassed in on one side to allow the police to watch their visitors if necessary. There was a table with a green cloth.

There were green velvet armchairs, a Louis-Philippe clock on the mantelpiece—the same as in Maigret's office, and in no better working order. Black frames on the walls held photographs of policemen who had fallen in the line of duty.

Two women huddled in armchairs, in a dark corner—Charlotte and Gigi.

In the corridor, on a bench, Prosper Donge—still without his tie and shoelaces—was sitting between two policemen.

"This way, Ramuel! Come into my office. And you, madame, please be good enough to sit in the waiting room for a minute. Show her the way, Lucas, my boy."

He opened the door to his office. He was smiling at the thought of the three women left alone in the waiting room, no doubt exchanging worried and angry glances.

"Come in, Ramuel! Do take off your overcoat, because it looks as though we'll be here for some time."

A green-shaded lamp threw its light on the table. Maigret took off his hat and coat, chose a pipe from his desk, and opened the door of the inspectors' room.

It was as if Police Headquarters, usually so empty at night, had been stuffed with people for the occasion. Torrence was sitting at his desk, with a felt hat on his head, smoking a cigarette; and across from him was a little old man with a ragged beard, staring with concentration at the elastic sides of his shoes.

Then there was Janvier, who had seized the chance to write up his report, and was also keeping an eye on a middle-aged man who looked as though he might once have been a noncommissioned officer in the army.

"Are you the concierge?" Maigret asked him. "Would you come into my office for a minute?"

Maigret stood aside to let him go in first. The man held his cap in his hand and didn't, at first, see Ramuel, who was standing as far from the light as possible.

"You're the concierge at 117b Rue Réaumur, aren't you? Some time ago a man called Prosper Donge rented one of your offices, and since then you have forwarded his mail to him. Do you recognize Donge?''

The concierge turned toward Ramuel in his corner, and shook his head, saying:

"Er . . . Frankly, I don't! I couldn't say for sure. I see so many people! And it was three years ago, wasn't it? I don't know if I remember rightly, but I have a vague idea that he had a beard. But perhaps the beard was someone else.''

"Thank you . . . You can go now. . . . This way . . .''

One down. Maigret opened the door again and called:

"Monsieur Jem! I don't know what your real name is. Come in, please. And would you be good enough to tell me . . .''

There was no need to wait for an answer this time. The little old man started with surprise on seeing Ramuel.

"Well?''

"Well what?''

"Do you recognize him?''

The old man was boiling.

"I'll have to go and give evidence at the trial, I suppose? And they'll leave me to rot for two or three days in the witnesses' room, and who'll look after my shop while I'm away? . . . Then, when I'm on the witness stand, I'll be asked a lot of embarrassing questions, and the lawyers will say a lot of things about me that will ruin my reputation. . . . No, thank you, Superintendent!''

Then he suddenly added:

"What's he done?''

"Well—he's killed two people, for a start—a man and a woman. The woman was a rich American. . . .''

"Is there a reward?''

"A pretty large one, yes . . .''

"In that case, take this down: '*I, Jean-Baptiste Meyer, businessman* . . .'" Will there be many witnesses sharing the reward? Because I know what happens. . . . The police make fine promises. . . . Then, when it comes to the point . . .'"

"I'll write: '. . . *formally recognize in the man presented to me as Jean Ramuel the person with whom I dealt at my private correspondence bureau under the initials J. M. D.*' Is that correct, Monsieur Meyer?"

"Where do I sign?"

"Wait! I'll add: '. . . *and I confirm that the said person came to collect a final letter on* . . .'" Now you can sign. You're a cunning old devil, Monsieur Meyer, because you know very well that all this will bring you a good deal of publicity, and that everyone who hadn't already heard of your bureau will be rushing to contact you. Torrence! Monsieur Meyer can go now."

When the door had shut behind him, the Superintendent read the repulsive old man's statement with satisfaction. A voice made him start. It came from a dark corner of the room—only the lamp on the desk was lighted.

"I protest, Superintendent, you . . ."

Then Maigret suddenly seemed to remember that he had forgotten something. He began by pulling the shade across the window. Then he looked at his hands. This was a Maigret that few people knew, and those who did didn't often boast about it afterward.

"Come over, Ramuel, my boy! Do as you're told, come here! Closer! Don't be afraid, now!"

"What are you . . . ?"

"You see, since I've discovered the truth, I've had a terrible urge to . . ."

As he spoke, Maigret's fist shot out and landed on the bookkeeper's nose, while, too late, Ramuel raised his arm.

166

"There! . . . It's against regulations, of course, but it does one good. Tomorrow, the judge will interrogate you politely and everyone will be nice to you, because you'll have become the star attraction of the court. Those gentlemen are always impressed by a star performer, if you see what I mean. . . . There's some water in the basin, in the closet. Wash yourself; you look disgusting like that. . . ."

Ramuel, bleeding profusely, washed himself as best he could.

"Let me see! . . . That's better! You're almost presentable. Torrence! Lucas! Janvier! Come on, boys. Bring in the ladies and gentlemen. . . ."

Even his colleagues were surprised to find him so much more elated than he usually was at the end of no matter how difficult a case. He had lighted another pipe. The first to enter, between two policemen, was Donge, who held his handcuffed hands clumsily in front of him.

"Have you got the key?" Maigret asked one of the men.

He unlocked the handcuffs, and an instant later they snapped shut around Ramuel's wrists, while Donge stared at him with almost comic stupefaction.

The Superintendent then noticed that Donge had neither tie nor shoelaces, and he ordered Ramuel's laces and his little black silk bow tie to be taken away.

"Come in, ladies. . . . Come in, Monsieur Clark. . . . I know you can't understand what we're saying, but I'm sure Monsieur Davidson will be kind enough to translate. Does everyone have a chair? Yes, Charlotte, you can go and sit next to Prosper. But I must ask you not to be too effusive for the time being.

"Is everyone here? . . . Shut the door, Torrence!"

"What has he done?" Madame Ramuel asked in her raucous voice.

"Please, you sit down, too, madame! I hate talking to people who are standing up. No, Lucas! Don't bother to put on the ceiling light. It's cozier like this. What has he done? He's gone on doing what he's been doing all his life: committing forgeries. And I bet that if he's married you and spent so many years with a poisonous creature like you, if you'll pardon me for being frank, it's because you've got a hold over him. And you've got a hold over him because you knew what he was up to in Guayaquil. There's a cable on its way, and another to the company headquarters in London. I know in advance what the answers will be."

And Marie offered, in her vile voice:

"Why don't you answer him, Jean? So the two hundred and eighty thousand francs and the trip to Brussels were true, then! . . ."

She had leaped up like a jack-in-the-box, and rushed toward him.

"Scoundrel! Thief! Scum! To think . . ."

"Calm yourself, madame. It's much better for you that he didn't tell you anything, because if he had done so, I would have been obliged to arrest you as an accomplice, not just in the forgery, but in a double crime."

From then on, an almost comic note was added to the proceedings. Clark, who kept his eyes on Maigret, kept leaning across to his lawyer to say a few words in English. Each time, the Superintendent looked at him, and he was sure that the American must be saying, in his own language:

"What's he saying?"

However, Maigret continued:

"As for you, my poor Charlotte, I have to tell you something that Prosper perhaps told you on the last evening he spent with you. . . . When you thought he had got over it and you told him about Mimi's letter and the story of the child, he hadn't got over it at all. He didn't say anything, but he set to work during his breaks, in his kitchen, as Ramuel has explained, writing long letters to his former mistress. . . ."

"Don't you remember, Donge? . . . Don't you recall the details?"

Donge didn't know what to reply. He couldn't understand what was going on, and kept looking around him with his big sky-blue eyes.

"I don't understand what you mean, sir. . . . "

"How many letters did you write?"

"Three . . ."

"And on at least one of the three occasions, weren't you disturbed by a telephone call? Weren't you summoned to go to the storekeeper to collect your rations for the next day?"

"Possibly . . . Yes . . . I think I probably was."

"And your letter stayed on your table, just opposite Ramuel's booth. Unlucky Ramuel's booth. Ramuel, who, his whole life long, has committed forgeries without ever making a fortune. To whom did you give your letters to be mailed?"

"The elevator boy. He took them up to the lobby, where there was a mailbox."

"So Ramuel could easily have intercepted them. And Mimi . . . Forgive me, Monsieur Clark . . . she is still Mimi to us. . . . After Mrs. Clark, as I should call her, had received in Detroit some letters from her ex-lover, in which he wrote mainly about his son, she then received other, more menacing letters—in the same handwriting and still signed Donge, but these letters demanded money. The new Donge wanted to be paid to keep silent."

"Oh, sir!" Prosper interrupted.

"Keep quiet, man, and for the love of God try to understand!

Because it's all very complex, I assure you. And it's proof yet again that Ramuel never had any luck. First he had to write to Mimi that you had changed your address, which was easy, because you hadn't said much in your letters about your new way of life. Then he rented the office on Rue Réaumur in the name of Prosper Donge. . . ."

"But . . ."

"You don't need any proof of identity to rent an office, and you are given any mail that arrives addressed to you. Unfortunately, the check Mimi sent was made out to Prosper Donge, and banks do ask that your papers be in order.

"I repeat, Ramuel is an artist in that line. But first of all he had to know that you would be having half to three quarters of an hour off, in the breakfast kitchen, opposite his glass booth, under his very eyes, so to speak, and that you would spend the break writing your letters.

"He suddenly sees you writing a letter to your bank to close your account, asking them to send the balance to Saint-Cloud.

"But it wasn't this letter that reached the Crédit Lyonnais. It was another letter, written by Ramuel, still in your handwriting, merely giving a change of address. In future, any letters to Donge were to be addressed to 117b Rue Réaumur.

"Then the check is sent, to be paid into the account. As for the eight hundred-odd francs that you got in Saint-Cloud, it was Ramuel who sent them to you in the bank's name.

"A cleverly worked out bit of dirty business, as you can see!

"So clever, in fact, that Ramuel, distrusting the address on Rue Réaumur, took the additional precaution of having his mail sent on from there to a box number.

"Who would be able to follow his tracks now?

"Then, however, the unexpected happens. Mimi comes to France. Mimi is staying at the Majestic. Any minute now,

Donge, the real Donge, may meet her and tell her that he has never tried to blackmail her, and . . ."

Charlotte couldn't take any more. She was crying, without quite knowing why, as she might have done when reading a sad story or watching a sentimental movie. Gigi whispered in her ear:

"Stop it! Stop it!"

And no doubt Clark was still mumbling to his lawyer:

"What's he saying?"

"As for Mrs. Clark's death," Maigret continued, "it was accidental. Ramuel, who had access to the hotel register, knew that she was at the Majestic. Donge didn't know this. He learned of it by chance, on overhearing a conversation in the personnel dining room.

"He wrote to her. He set a meeting for six in the morning and probably wanted to demand that he be given his son, to beg her on his knees, to beseech her. . . . I'm sure that if they had met, Mimi would have run circles around him again. . . .

"He didn't know that, thinking she was about to meet a blackmailer, she had bought a gun.

"Ramuel was worried. He didn't leave the Majestic basement. The note Donge had sent via a bellboy had escaped his notice.

"And there it was! . . . A flat tire . . . Donge is a quarter of an hour late. . . . Ramuel sees the young woman wandering along the corridor in the basement and guesses what has happened, he is afraid that everything will come out. . . .

"He strangles her . . . pushes her into a locker. . . .

"He soon realizes that everything will point to Donge, and that there is nothing, in fact, that could possibly incriminate him.

"To make doubly certain of this, he writes an anonymous letter, in Charlotte's handwriting. Because there are several notes from Charlotte in the drawer in the breakfast kitchen.

"I repeat, he's a consummate artist! Meticulous! He takes care

171

of every detail! And when he realizes that poor Justin Colleboeuf, on his way to get his coffee, has seen him and will give him away, he commits another crime, with no trouble at all, and one that can easily be attributed to Donge.

"That is all. . . . Torrence! Use a damp towel on that scum—his nose is beginning to bleed again. He slipped just now and banged his face on the corner of the table.

"Have you anything to say, Ramuel?"

Silence. Only the American was still asking:

"What's he saying?"

"As for you, madame . . . What shall I call you? Marie Deligeard? Madame Ramuel?"

"I prefer Marie Deligeard."

"That's what I thought. You weren't mistaken in thinking he hoped to leave you soon. No doubt he was waiting until there was a nice round sum in the bank. Then he could go and look after his liver alone, abroad, a long way from your shouting and screaming."

"How dare you . . ."

"With all due respect, madame! With all due respect!"

And suddenly, to the policemen:

"Take the prisoner to the cells. I hope that tomorrow Examining Magistrate Bonneau will be good enought to sign a final warrant and that . . ."

Gigi was standing in a corner, perched on her stiltlike legs; all the emotion had given her such a craving for drugs that she felt dizzy, and her nostrils fluttered like a wounded bird's wings.

"Excuse me, Superintendent. . . ."

It was the lawyer. Clark stood behind him.

"My client would like to have a meeting with you, Monsieur Donge, and himself, in my office, as soon as possible, to discuss

. . . to discuss the child who . . ."

"D'you hear that, Prosper?" cried Gigi triumphantly, from her corner.

"Would tomorrow morning suit you? Are you free tomorrow morning, Monsieur Donge?"

But Donge couldn't speak. He had suddenly cracked. He had thrown himself on Charlotte's ample bosom and was crying, crying his heart out, as the saying goes, while, a little embarrassed, she soothed him like a child.

"Pull yourself together, Prosper! We'll bring him up together! We'll teach him French. We'll . . ."

Maigret—God knows why—was rummaging through the drawers of his desk. He remembered that he had put some glassine envelopes taken during a recent raid in one of them. He took one out, hesitated a moment, shrugged.

Then, just as Gigi was at the point of fainting, he brushed past her. His hand touched hers.

"Ladies and gentlemen, it's one in the morning. Be so kind . . ."

"*What's he saying?*" Clark seemed still to be asking, at the end of his first encounter with the French police.

They learned the following morning that the check for two hundred and eighty thousand francs had been presented at the Société Générale in Brussels, by a man named Jaminet, a bookmaker by profession.

Jaminet had received it by airmail from Ramuel, who had been his superior during his military service, when he was a corporal.

Which didn't keep Ramuel from denying everything to the last.

Or from being lucky for the first time in his life, because, owing to his poor state of health—he fainted three times during the final hearing—his death sentence was commuted to hard labor for life.

Nieul-sur-Mer, 1939